"You're furious with me, aren't you?"

"Yes, Venus." Eli pulled her into his arms. "Did you think I wanted to be wrapped in silk bows while you put yourself in harm's way?"

"No, but—"

"No excuses. Anything that threatens you is my business. Whether you take me or leave me, I'll always care for you."

"I—I wouldn't ever leave for good." Tears clogged her throat. "Don't you know that I couldn't risk getting you involved in this mess? It's my problem, and I thought I could handle it alone." Her words feathered his mouth as she nuzzled close to him.

"Don't you know I want to be there for you, to be your support, your buffer?" His lips gently touched her brow, sending electric shivers through her.

The world faded away as passion took them, enflaming their hearts with a raging firestorm.

"I guess I'm a fool," she whispered.

His voice was a growl. "Yes. But you're my fool, Venus. And I'll never let you go."

HELEN MITTERMEYER

Golden Touch

PAGEANT BOOKS

PAGEANT BOOKS
225 Park Avenue South
New York, New York 10003

Cover artwork by Renato Aime

Printed in the U.S.A.

First Pageant Books printing: November, 1988

10 9 8 7 6 5 4 3 2 1

To my husband, who is my friend, inspiration, and lover, and to my children, Paul, Ann, Dan, and Christy, who have stood by me and cheered me on.

Golden Touch

Chapter One

Life could be a kick in the head, but Venus Wayne was fighting back.

Her job as a messenger was hardly fulfilling, but it paid the bills. Although the salary wasn't a quarter of what she'd made as a partner in her own investment firm, the money helped pay off the substantial debts she'd inherited. And once she had a less expensive apartment, she wouldn't have to struggle to get the rent together each month.

Venus smiled to herself at the assorted glances cast her way as she skated across the lobby. After a month on the job, she was used to such looks.

The Weldon-Tate Building, headquarters for one of the world's largest conglomerates, was huge and required fast mail delivery from floor to floor and person to person. Roller skates provided a handy, speedy way to get around.

At first the job had seemed so alien to Venus. It was a far cry from her vocation as an investment counselor at Teague and Wayne. But after the shattering collapse of her small company, she'd been glad to get any job that would keep her close to Wall Street and the world she loved. Venus would have taken the position of street sweeper if it had been the only one available on Wall Street.

Maneuvering past a woman with a child, she

couldn't help hearing the high-pitched observations of the little girl.

"Mommy, that lady has a big sack, just like our mailman. Can I get skates like that?"

Venus smiled at the girl, then glided across the lobby. She had deliveries to make—that had to be her focus for the moment. Eventually, she would find a position in the business world. She faced a slow, steady struggle, but one day she would have her own firm again. For now she would deliver mail and keep her ears open. There was much to learn from the business glitterati at Weldon-Tate.

Venus had promised herself that she wouldn't look back; she wouldn't dwell on the past. Having used up all her savings to pay the debts of her now defunct company, she was in a precarious financial position. But she was alive and healthy, unlike poor Jeremy, her former partner. Venus Wayne had hit rock bottom . . . but there was nowhere to go but up.

"Dammit, I won't sit here and have my ability to run this company questioned. Yes, we lost money on Black Monday, but we did not take a beating. We are not down for the count. It's only been four weeks since the crash and already we are back on keel. Everyone here knows that." Eli Weldon-Tate leaped to his feet, glaring from one board member to another.

But their faces were unresponsive. Realizing the futility of boxing with shadows, he threw down his pen. "This meeting is adjourned for an hour. I'm going downstairs to get coffee."

"There's coffee *here*, Eli," Dismas Weldon, his uncle, said dryly.

"We all need a break from this," Eli said tersely.

"Eli, wait," Benedict James, his lawyer, said warningly.

Eli ignored the protests and stormed from the boardroom. He had to get out of there before he put his fist through a wall . . . or through the cynical sneer of a board member.

The image of those staid investors knocked out cold gave him an odd sense of satisfaction as his private elevator sped him to the lobby.

Eli was more than a little irked; he was downright furious. The board meeting had turned into an angry confrontation, the members castigating him for the losses suffered by the Black Monday crash of October, even though the firm had already begun to recoup. Damn them! He'd cut his teeth on the Street with bigger deals than they'd ever faced. Did they think he was some callow youth in the market? That he wouldn't have backup plans in case of emergency?

His lawyer had tried to convince him that restraint was his best bet, but Eli was sick of pandering to critics and so-called advisors. Patience wasn't his strong suit, even at the best of times. Today he was ready to blow his top.

"Damn," he muttered as he punched the elevator button yet again. He'd fought hard to maintain his position as CEO—and even harder to maintain the high standards of Weldon-Tate. Eli had broken his back to save the company from a hostile takeover, yet his ability to manage the firm was still questioned. Each board meeting was like a bout of hand-to-hand combat, and Eli was getting sick of the constant battle. War was hell.

Even his uncle, Eli's only family, seemed concerned by some of his nephew's methods. Once CEO of Weldon-Tate, Dismas didn't welcome all the changes Eli had implemented. Eli knew he would eventually win his uncle's support, but it cut him to think that his own family was joining the treasonous board.

Hadn't Eli improved the Weldon-Tate legacy?

He was a fool to feel so threatened. When he cooled down a bit, he would discuss the situation with his uncle and his lawyer, the only advisors he could really trust.

Eli had known Benedict James since prep school days. Although they hadn't been friends back then, an easy camaraderie had developed after Benedict replaced his deceased father, whose law firm had represented Weldon-Tate for years. And though he was one of the newest members of the board, Benedict had spoken in Eli's defense.

Not that it had done any good. An even more heated argument had ensued, prompting Eli to bang his gavel and call a recess before tempers exploded.

Intent on getting a cup of coffee and walking off his ire, Eli stepped from the elevator to the main foyer of the huge Weldon-Tate Building.

As he walked across the polished marble floor, his eyes roved the multistoried atrium of the modern complex, a wonder of steel and glass. Rivers of people thronged through the spacious lobby, which spanned from one side of the block to the other.

Eli's fury gave way to a thrust of pride. The sight of this building, a monument to his family's achievements, always helped him put his priorities in order.

The teeming crowd seemed to dissipate around Eli, though a lovely red-haired messenger skated dangerously close. His glance lingered for a moment on the tall, lithe young woman before he was distracted by a flicker of light from above.

He glanced up at the strange but unmistakable sight. Was that a rifle poking from the shadows of the fifth-floor atrium?

Eli froze, unable to believe his own eyes. Then he was galvanized into action.

It was a gun. And the pretty, red-headed messenger was directly in the line of fire.

The first shot was the merest sound in the hub-bub of people.

Eli dived through the air a millisecond before the shot, reaching for the skating messenger. Still in flight, he caught the woman, bringing her down so that his body struck the ground first. Then he rolled over on top of her.

"W-what are you doing?" she gasped.

"Stay still."

The woman tried to free herself, still unaware of the shot and the crowd that had begun to scatter around them. "Look, if this is some sort of new come-on, I'm not buying it. Do you hear me?"

Eli continued to scan the atrium. Where the hell was the gunman now? "Don't move. He might start shooting again." When he felt the sudden slackness in the body beneath him, Eli assumed that she was eyeing the lobby, too.

"What's going on here?" Venus began to notice that the people around them were rushing for cover, and a sharp, icy fear crept up her spine. "God!"

Eli's blood ran cold through his veins when he heard another telltale crack of a bullet thudding close to him. His experience in Vietnam told him that the shot was close. But this was no jungle. What the hell was going on?

Grasping the woman to his side, he edged across the floor, moving as fast as he could to the protection of a monstrous marble column.

Venus was amazed at the strength of the man holding her. She no longer protested, realizing that he was pulling her away from the line of fire.

Releasing her, the powerful man moved slowly to his knees and shouted into the melee of baffled and frightened people. "Everyone stay down. Remain under cover until security—" His words were cut off by gunfire. A slug shattered a glass panel into crystalline slivers.

People crouched and scattered as fearful murmurs filled the air.

Again the gun fired.

Just above Eli's head a bullet plowed into the marble column, scattering shards of stone. A marble sliver stung his cheek. Eli moved back, scooping the young woman into his arms without thinking, using the column as a shield.

"You're bleeding," she said.

"Shh, it's all right." Eli's arms tightened around her. Although his mind never strayed from the situation at hand, an errant thought confirmed his first impression of the skating messenger. She had a slender, beautiful body.

Time had no measure. Silence touched with sighs and sobbings was the only reality. There was no movement.

Then there was a crashing noise and the unmistakable sounds of action. As blue-coated security guards moved swiftly into position, the gleaming steel barrel of the gun vanished from sight.

Venus reached up and gently touched the man's cheek, the velvet toughness causing a fluttering feeling in her middle. What a wonderful, rugged face he had. "Are you all right?" she asked, feeling a strong urge to tend to the wounded cheek herself.

"Thank you." Eli smiled down at her, noting the

slight tremor in her hands. No screams, recrimina-
tions, or tears. This woman was beautiful *and* gutsy.
Cold sweat beaded his body at the thought of what
a rifle bullet could have done to her.

As Eli helped the woman to her feet, he recalled
the slim but rounded body he'd just held in his
arms. "And what about you? Are you all right?"
His gaze touched her from eyebrow to ankle and
back again. Tall, lovely . . . and a tad too slim.

"I'm okay," she said as she dusted off her sleeves
and started retrieving the scattered envelopes and
periodicals.

She did have a very rounded backside . . . wonderful, tempting. That red hair had escaped her
messenger cap and was now rioting around her
shoulders. And her eyes were amazing—a deep,
warm violet.

Although Eli found her captivating, his brain
was still fixed on the gunman. Who the hell was
it? And why was he shooting? Who had been the
target? His glance sliced away from the lovely
messenger. Was his imagination in overdrive, or
could he have been the target? Dammit! He was
going to get some answers.

Focusing on this urgent matter, Eli turned to the
head of security. "Merriman, I want to talk to you
and to the head of the police SWAT team."

"Yes, sir, right this way."

Venus looked up from the floor where she was
gathering the mail, watching the man in the finely
tailored suit as he strode toward a group of police-
men. He had broad shoulders and moved like an
athlete. Rugged and rich. Did he have an office in
the Weldon-Tate building?

One uniformed cop approached her as she tucked
a handful of envelopes into her bag. "Pardon me,
miss. I'd like to get a statement from you."

"All right, officer, but it will have to be fast. I'm late now, and I don't want to lose my job." How could she answer so calmly when her insides were churning? A maniac had been firing a gun in her direction! It was macabre—unbelievable!

With a deep breath, she tried to calm herself, then answered the questions as best she could. Unfortunately, she hadn't seen much. "Ah, that's really all I remember, officer." She was afraid her account wasn't too helpful. She'd seen the gun but not the person. "It all happened so fast," she explained.

"Thank you, ma'am."

"You're welcome." Venus scooped up the last of the mail, stuffed it into her bag, and flung the pouch over her shoulder. She would have to hustle since her schedule was now way off.

She still couldn't believe that someone really had fired a gun in the Weldon-Tate Building. She shivered, then stole one last glance at the tall, rugged-looking man with the no-nonsense green eyes. She owed him her life and yet didn't even know his name. Too bad they hadn't met at another time, under different circumstances.

Pushing off on her skates, she moved into the throng. In seconds, she'd disappeared in the midday crush of people meandering through the concourse. Disappearing in the mass of people was easy . . . even for a gunman.

"I want some answers and I want them fast!" Eli demanded.

"Mr. Tate, I assure you that my people will comb the area and try to find the sniper as soon as possible. Do you think you were the target?"

Eli exhaled. "I don't know. Maybe. There was a messenger over there . . ." Eli turned but saw no one. "She's gone."

"Don't worry, sir. If she was here, one of our people questioned her."

"Fine. Get back to me on this. Merriman, as head of security I want you on top of this. I'll be in my office. Report to me as soon as you have anything."

"Yes, sir."

With a nod, Eli strode across the concourse toward the elevator bank. For the first time in memory, he regretted that his family owned this enormous building with the capacity to hold such a large crowd. Anything could happen in such a spacious public place.

Could the messenger have been the target? It didn't make sense. Could that beautiful, intriguing creature really have a mortal enemy?

Had it been an eon or merely minutes since he'd stepped from the elevator and looked up into the atrium?

As he pushed his key into the lock to activate the elevator, the lovely messenger girl bloomed in his mind. He was haunted by the woman, the leather messenger cap askew over her forehead. She was like a nettle under his skin. Was it coincidence that she'd been there when the shots were fired? Was he the target? Or was she? The gunman could have been firing random shots into the crowd, but Eli had a gut feeling that wasn't the case.

In his office, he cleaned the cut on his face, then buzzed his secretary. When she told him that the board had canceled the rest of the meeting, he said, "Good. Get me the mail room, please." He dropped into his swivel chair and lifted the phone when it buzzed. "Hello, Sandy? Do you have a red-haired messenger about five feet ten and ... What? Her name is Venus Wayne? Really? Ah, no, but could you have her deliver my mail immediately. No, there's not a problem with the other messenger. I would like Miss . . . Wayne to deliver my mail—right away. You can tell her to use my private elevator. Thanks, Sandy."

He scowled when his secretary buzzed him again. "Mr. James is here to see you."

"All right. Send him in."

Eli stood and faced his longtime acquaintance and business associate. "I thought you'd already gone back to your office, Ben."

Benedict James had his main office a few blocks away, but, as a lawyer for the firm, he also maintained an office at Weldon-Tate's. Because of this, he often seemed a fixture of the corporation.

"I wanted to check on you first. I understand I missed a bit of excitement in the lobby."

"That's a nice way to describe bedlam. It was nasty down there. We were lucky no one was killed."

"Another disenchanted investor?"

"Could be. I'll know more when I get Merriman's report. So? What did you want to say?"

"Eli, I think it's time we made a move. Half of the board members are sitting on the fence waiting to be persuaded. I thought—"

Ben was interrupted by the red button flashing on the console. "You have someone coming up in the private elevator, Eli?"

"Yes," he said, nodding distractedly.

Ben grinned. "From the look on your face, I assume you'd like some privacy."

Eli nodded. "Put your proposal in writing, and I'll look at it in the morning."

Benedict flipped his two fingers off his forehead in salute, then pointed to the flashing light. "Better get that. Talk to you tomorrow," he said as he left the room.

Eli pressed the elevator release, then resumed his seat, steepling his hands in front of him. Maybe he was crazy to summon her to his office. What could this woman tell him, anyway? Neither one of them had seen the sniper. And yet for some reason he had to see that violet-eyed woman once more . . .

The door swung open and she stood there, a mail bag in her hands, skates still on her feet. The words slipped out as her eyes widened in recognition. "Oh, hello."

"Hello." Eli rose to his feet. She was even more beautiful than he remembered. "How are you feeling?"

"Better. How's the cut on your face?"

Eli's hand went to the mark now covered by a small bandage. "It's fine, thank you."

Venus nodded, still wondering why he had called her here. Did he intend to fire her? No, he would let somebody else handle that. She'd lost some of his mail! No, he wasn't on her route.

"I was wondering, Miss Wayne, if you had managed to garner any enemies who might want to shoot you down?"

"Me? Certainly not." She had paid off the debts her company had accrued, and she had the empty bankbook as well as a loan payment book to prove it. "Do *you* have enemies?" She could have bitten off her tongue for asking that, and when he didn't answer, she murmured, "Sorry. I had a bad day."

"So did I," Eli drawled, watching the coloration of her eyes turn from violet to purple as she became more agitated.

Licking her suddenly dry lips, she recalled the strength of that hard body when he'd held her in the lobby. For a flash of time she'd felt cherished, protected, an alien sensation in her life.

"It was a frightening time down in the lobby," he offered.

"Yes." Had he read her mind?

Venus needed time to regroup. The man who'd been imprinted on her brain since she'd parted from him was now standing in Eli Weldon-Tate's office. It was safe to assume she'd been tackled by the head of Weldon-Tate Enterprises. "I don't know what more I can tell you about the sniper. I gave my statement to the police, Mr. . . . er . . . Weldon-Tate." Had she ever seen his picture before? Probably. He was always in *Business Week* or some such periodical. But photographs didn't convey charisma—or electric green eyes.

Eli approached her and took her arm. "Why don't I help you remove those skates, and we can discuss what happened in the lobby?" Eli maneuvered her into the nearest chair and kneeled in front of her.

"I should get back to work. I have a tight delivery schedule to keep." Her leg tingled where his hand had brushed it.

From his position on the floor, Eli raised his head to study the violet eyes looking down into his. "We were in grave danger today. You need to relax." He reached for the lace of her right skate, but suddenly stopped. "Venus," he murmured. "Who gave you the name of the mythical goddess of love and beauty?"

She laughed. "My father wanted to call me Aphrodite, but mother held firm." Her eyes locked on his bandaged cheek. What would it be like to kiss the rugged jawline, the high cheekbone? She straightened in her chair, looking toward the elevator. "I have to go."

"Would you have preferred Aphrodite?"

"No. I'm not sure I can spell it."

When Eli saw the dimple at the side of her mouth flash, his insides went into a tailspin. "Would you like a job on this floor, Venus?" Where had that impulse come from? He knew only that he wanted to be near this woman, to get a chance to know her.

"If people heard you offering a clerical job to a messenger, they would really think you'd lost your mind."

"Probably, but they don't run this company, I do."

Venus rose from the chair. "I had better get back to work. I still have a mountain of mail to get rid of before quitting time." Her lopsided smile touched him like a brand.

Eli felt chagrined. Why not allow her to disappear and forget he'd ever seen her? No, that would be impossible to do. "Will you at least consider my offer?"

"Yes, but I don't think I'll be taking it." Her body heated at the thought of seeing Eli Weldon-Tate every day on the job. "And I think you'll regret making the offer as soon as I'm out of here." She dropped his mail onto his desk and cocked her head inquiringly at him. "And as soon as you find out who I *really* am."

Chapter Two

*T*houghts of Eli Weldon-Tate crowded in Venus's mind during the bus ride to her apartment on the second floor of a brownstone. The quaint, homey apartment had been affordable last year when her investment firm had been growing and thriving. But that was before the fall. Before the Black Monday stock market crash, before the firm had encountered financial trouble, and before the untimely death of her partner, Jeremy Teague. It was hard to believe that laughing, mercurial Jeremy was gone! And it still hurt to think of it.

She loved her apartment, but she had no illusions about staying there much longer; the rent was too steep. Mrs. Wallader, her landlady, was a supreme pragmatist and would be quick to ask Venus to leave once she got behind in the payments.

When she unlocked the door to the front foyer, her landlady appeared as though Venus had conjured her up.

"Miss Wayne." The heavyset landlady seemed serious. "I consider myself as liberal as the next person."

"Yes?" Venus racked her brain for some infraction.

"I do not mind you entertaining friends, but I think when you are not here, that sort of partying is out of line and I want no more of it."

"What party? When?"

"I'm sure you would know more about that than I would, Miss Wayne," Mrs. Wallader said primly, then disappeared into her own apartment, her yapping dog, Mimi, at her heels.

"That woman!" Venus murmured, still baffled. Stomping up to the second floor, she unlocked her door and pulled it open.

The sight that met her eyes flummoxed her. The few bits of furniture that Venus hadn't as yet sold were smashed and torn. The apartment was a shambles. Legs torn from tables, drawers upended and broken, lamps leaning drunkenly.

It was too much! She'd been shot at, tackled to the ground, and now this! Life was a nasty circus. She'd lost her business, her partner, her savings, her . . .

"Oh, no! Tweety!" Tears coursed from her eyes when she looked at the dead cockateel in its cage. The bird had been so precious to her. Everything was gone. All she had left of any value was a safety deposit box in her bank: a sapphire ring inherited from her grandmother and a cryptic notebook Jeremy had left to her. There had been nothing of any value in the ledger, but it was in Jeremy's handwriting so she'd kept it. It was all she had of him.

As though in a trance, she went to the phone and dialed the police. Twice in one day she would give them a statement, this time in her own home.

When his houseman spoke to him, Eli responded absently, staring into his liqueur glass in fixed concentration.

"Ya barely touched your supper."

Eli frowned at Kelly Monihan, the man who ran his household like a finely tuned instrument. "I have a lot on my mind."

Monihan glared at him. "Ya mean the shooting?"

"Among other things. I'll have more coffee." How was Venus Wayne bearing up after her bizarre day?

"Help yourself. It's in the pot in front of you." Monihan stomped from the dining room to his sanctum, the kitchen.

How was Venus Wayne faring? Eli wondered. The woman seemed to have courage, but it had been a harrowing day for everyone.

Was the shooting tied to her? Or was someone trying to take him out? These questions had turned around and around in his mind all day, and they probably would continue to until he found some answers.

It was strange that he should literally run into a woman who filled his brain with so many unanswered questions . . . and who intrigued him as no female had done in some time.

Business had filled his life since he'd taken over Weldon-Tate. Women were an attractive addendum to that life, but no one had really taken his focus from the firm. Only his Uncle Dismas had been able to penetrate the armor he'd developed during childhood. Business had become the only occupation Eli needed. Until today. He refilled his coffee cup, his shoulders shifting uneasily. Why should a messenger on skates—

Rising abruptly to his feet, he almost knocked his chair backward. "Monihan! I'm going out." Eli was almost out of the dining room when his houseman poked his head into the room.

"And will ya be back?"

"I usually am."

"Usually, but not always."

All the way down in the elevator to the underground garage, Eli castigated himself. Why in hell was he going to her place? In fact, why had he bothered to bring up her personnel file on the computer that afternoon? Was it that cryptic remark she'd made about discovering her true identity?

Pulling a sheet of paper from his pocket, he slid behind the wheel of his sleek Ferrari and once more studied her address. It wasn't a long ride to Venus Wayne's apartment.

Eli drove through Manhattan, not noticing the magic kaleidoscope of New York at night. Most of the time the city gave him great satisfaction. Though he had a country estate in upstate New York, the city always beckoned to him. He had known from adolescence that he would challenge Wall Street when it came time for him to make his way in the world.

With the fortune left by his parents, plus shares in Weldon-Tate, he'd parlayed his business instincts and knowledge into an investment empire. Now, all of it was in danger of collapsing like a deck of cards. And rumors were the weapons being used to destroy him. Innuendo was his enemy, and it all seemed to stem from the board members. "It won't happen. I won't let it!" He hit the steering wheel with his fist.

Checking the address on the computer printout once more, Eli pulled up in front of an apartment house. It was in a safe if unpretentious neighborhood, too high-priced for a messenger to handle on her salary.

Eli frowned. Did she live with someone? A man? He reached for the ignition key to restart his car, then paused.

The hell with it! He might as well see for himself rather than speculate all night.

After getting out of his car, he stared at the brick facade for long moments.

In a second-floor window, curtains moved. Although Eli saw Venus Wayne, he knew she didn't see him. Her forehead was pressed against the glass in a forlorn, sad posture. Was she crying?

Striding across the sidewalk, he took the cement steps two at a time to the small entrance vestibule. VENUS WAYNE, APARTMENT 2B. He pressed the bell under her name and heard her voice almost at once crackling over the speaker. "It's Eli Weldon-Tate. May I come up?" The long hesitation after the sharply indrawn breath irked him. He was about to turn back when the door release sounded.

He walked up the long staircase that hugged one wall. As he reached the upper hallway, her door opened.

"Hello, Mr. Weldon-Tate. Why are you here?"

Eli saw the surreptitious swipe at a stray tear. "Are you all right?"

Her violet eyes were clouded with pain and confusion. "I don't know what I feel at the moment."

"May I come in?"

Reluctantly, Venus moved to one side. "It's still a mess. The police only left a short—"

"Police? Why were they . . . ?" Eli's voice trailed off as he looked at the upended furniture. "You've had a burglary?"

"Astute of you," she said sarcastically, then sighed, massaging her forehead with two fingers. "Sorry. I'm on edge." Actually she was coming apart at the seams, flying to pieces like a bad watch. What was she going to do?

"You can't stay here. Come to my place. I have plenty of room. You'd have your own portion of the place. No strings." The damned girl seemed to control his impulses.

Venus shook her head.

"Look, be sensible. You'd be up most of the night trying to put this in order. Even if you did get to bed, chances are your imagination would keep you awake. Come to my place, and tomorrow, early, we'll get a cleaning crew in here to—"

"It's okay. I'll be moving, anyway."

"All the more reason to stay at my place. You'll have your own locks and—"

"They killed my cockateel!" Tears spilled from her eyes. "No! Don't—don't be nice to me." Venus held her hands up, palms outward. "I'll—I'll be fine. I don't know why I'm crying."

"Maybe you need to." Eli clenched his hands at his sides, wanting to sweep her up in his arms and carry her down to his car. Yet he didn't move. "Here. Take my handkerchief."

Venus dabbed at her eyes with it and blew her nose hard.

"Now will you get some things together and come with me?"

She looked at the shambles surrounding her.

"I give you my word that you have nothing to fear from me, Miss Wayne."

"I probably should get it in writing," she mumbled. Then, noting the play of blood as it rose in his face, she amended, "I've insulted you again. I'm sorry."

"No, it's all right," Eli said abruptly. "I'll just have to learn to bob and weave better. But if you'd been a man, I'd have landed you one."

"If I'd been a man, you wouldn't be here." Blood was beginning to flow through her again.

Damn her! He should leave now before she completely made a fool of him. "Get some things together, Venus," he said firmly, brooking no argument.

But she was not easily swayed. For a long moment she stared at him, then said, "I'll think about it. Excuse me while I splash some cold water on my face." She turned around and strode down a short hall.

Eli studied the cluttered room. Could it be a coincidence? Maybe. But this eerie burglary followed too closely behind the shooting. What the hell was going on? What had the intruders stolen from her? He looked up as she returned to him. "Did they take much?"

Venus shrugged. "I'm not sure. Nothing much seems to be missing. They just . . . destroyed things." She shook her head. She had already sold her valuable jewelry and furniture to pay the bills that Teague and Wayne had accrued.

Suddenly Eli was nearly overwhelmed by anger laced with fear. What if she had come home while the intruders were still here? "You're coming to my place." His abrupt remark brought her head up sharply.

"Don't play tough-guy with me." She bit her lip when her voice ended squeakily.

"You can't stay here." If he had to pick her up and toss her over his shoulder, he would do it. She wasn't staying in this apartment.

"Won't living in the same house as you be like entering an arena?"

"We'll call a truce. Starting now." Eli put out his hand. When she shook it, a jolt of warmth shot through him.

Wriggling free of his grip, she said, "Let me throw some clothes together and we'll be off."

It didn't take her long to pack. A moment later he took the bag from her hand. "Shall we go?" He didn't miss the tiny shudder that went through her when she took one last look at the living room. "Sure there's not some memento you'd like to bring?"

Venus shook her head, her glance lingering on the empty gilt bird cage hanging askew on its chain. The police had been kind enough to take the dead bird away, so at least she had been spared that unpleasant task.

They were silent as they walked down the long, wide staircase to the foyer. As they passed, a door on the first floor opened. "Miss Wayne? I thought I heard your door close. Are you feeling better? Are the police gone?"

Venus nodded, though a haunted look lingered in her eyes. "I'll be back very early, Mrs. Wallader."

"I've already rented your place, and the new tenants will be moving in on Friday."

Eli put the small suitcase on the floor and removed some bills from a money clip. "Will that hold her things until the movers get here in the morning?"

"That's too much," Venus objected.

"That will be fine." Mrs. Wallader clutched the bills, then scuttled back into her apartment.

"Why, the cagey old beetle! And I wasn't really that far in arrears." Venus glared at the landlady's door.

"Let's go. I'll arrange for your things to be cleared out in the morning."

"I'll just be staying overnight," she reminded him. "I'll look for a place on my lunch hour."

"That's up to you."

They went down the wide cement steps to the sidewalk.

Venus stared at his Ferrari. "I sold my car."

"A great many people suffered from the crash, I understand."

"But not you."

"Not me," he said cautiously. "Not yet."

The drive to his apartment was executed in stiff silence, the nighttime sounds of the city providing a cacophonous echo in the brooding quiet.

When they reached the underground garage, Eli drove to his reserved parking spot and turned off the ignition. Then he faced the woman who had stared blankly through the windshield during the entire drive. "You've had a rough time. I shouldn't have been sparring with you that way after the day you've had. I'm sorry."

Venus didn't look at him. "You offered me a night's lodging. And I do appreciate that." Her gaze shifted in his direction by a degree. "We've had a few bad starts. Right?"

"That's for sure. Most people don't have to dodge gunfire the first time they meet." Her breathy chuckle ran over his skin like feathery kisses.

"Did they get the gunman?" she asked, wondering what else could go wrong today. It took all of her strength just to stem the shudders that threatened to wrack her body. What a hell of a day!

"The preliminary police report indicates that either you or I were the target of a sniper." Eli watched her head swivel his way. The dim, yellowish garage light delineated the shock and anger that flashed across her face.

"That's crazy. Well, I mean, not for you, maybe, but for me. I've paid my debts—well, most of them—and I haven't collected enemies along the way."

"Then *I* must have been the target," he said consolingly. But Eli knew that Venus Wayne could be wrong about having enemies. According to her dossier, she'd started her own business, and that was a surefire way to lose a few friends. "Tell me about the company you had." He smiled at her surprised expression. "Your personnel file says you had a small investment firm that folded."

"Jeremy and I started it on a shoestring and prayer shortly after we got out of business school in Syracuse. That's where we met." Venus sighed. "Normally we could have ridden out a crisis like Black Monday. I didn't realize we were so badly overextended."

Eli touched a tendril of hair that curled atop her shoulder. "Older and wiser investors than you went down, Venus."

"I know."

He waited a moment, watching the play of emotions on her features, made surreal by the dim lights. He had a sense that she regretted telling him as much as she had, though she hadn't been that forthcoming with information. "Do you like the messenger work at Weldon-Tate?"

Venus looked at him for the first time, a smile flitting over her face. "Actually, I do. It helps me forget about Jeremy and all the events of the last few weeks. And the exercise is great," she finished lamely.

"And you're close to the business that interests you."

Venus shrugged. "The business is in my blood. But I'm afraid it will be some time before I can work my way back up again. I'll keep my ear to the ground for possibilities, of course, but right now I have bills to pay. After that I'll think about . . . other things."

Eli watched her for a moment longer. Even in the faint light he could tell that her face was pale; her lower lip trembled ever so slightly. "Let's get out of this car. It's getting cold."

Venus walked beside him to the elevator, then watched as he inserted his key. The illuminated console contained numbers from one to thirty.

Eli pressed the button marked *P*.

When they reached the penthouse, he again inserted his key and the doors opened into a caramel-hued marble foyer.

"Quite a security system," Venus murmured, stepping into the spacious area and looking around her.

He opened the drawer of a delicate rosewood table in the foyer and took out a key, which he then handed to her. "This is yours. It also fits the back service elevator and allows you access to the stairway if you feel inclined to walk down thirty stories."

Venus stared at the key, then took it from him. "Thank you."

"Now, let's look at your room. Then we'll have something to eat. You probably didn't have dinner."

She shrugged. "I forgot about it."

Eli smiled at the look of surprise on her face. Without thinking, he reached out and touched her cheek with one finger. "I make a great omelet."

"Shouldn't I be the judge of that?" Suddenly out of breath, she walked away from him. Could he tell that her insides had just turned to jelly? Eli Weldon-Tate was a world-class hunk and he was quite aware of it, probably. From the moment they'd collided in the lobby, he'd had an unsettling effect on her. As her gaze wandered over the luxurious furnishings, a grouping of photographs caught her eye. One featured a young Eli in athletic attire. Another captured him sparring with a brawny opponent. "So you were a boxer?"

"If you are referring to my crooked nose, I got

that when I was racing, though I did a little boxing at the university."

"A jock, by God," Venus murmured, laughing.

"You could say that." Eli linked his arm with
hers. "Let me show you your room."

"It's a beautiful apartment."

"There are three floors and a terrace." Eli led
her up the curving staircase to a short hall. Pointing to the foyer that led to another wing, he said,
"Those are my quarters over there. This is yours.
As you can see, you have total privacy."

"Thank you, sir, for protecting my person," Venus
said in a little-girl voice.

"You can be very caustic, Miss Wayne."

How could Venus describe the giddy relief she
felt in his company? It was insane. She was in a
stranger's apartment, but she'd never felt as safe
with anyone, at any time, as she did at that moment. Walking into a den of lions would have been
cannier, but her body and mind sagged with the
release of the tension she'd been carrying.

Eli Weldon-Tate had a power and strength that
magnetized her. She knew she should run and
never look back. But somehow, for some reason
she couldn't define, Venus found herself falling
under the spell of this formidable man.

He was offering her protection for one night. But
who would protect her from the charms of Eli
Weldon-Tate? Venus wondered as she followed him
down the hall.

He threw open a large oak door, and Venus gazed
into the spacious room. "Louis Quinze, isn't it?"

"Yes, you have a good eye for design. My grandmother, who decorated this place, liked that pe-
riod. The petite rococo style appealed to her, and
she liked the comfort of it. Do you like it?"

Venus nodded, her hair swirling around her as she swiveled to take in the whole room. Then she faced Eli, who was propped against the doorjamb. "I think I would have liked to have known your grandmother." When she saw the flash of pain on his face, she inclined her head.

"My grandmother was the original grande dame, but there was no one with a kinder heart."

"And your mother and father? Brothers and sisters?"

"I'm an only child, and my parents are dead," he told her abruptly. "Do I get the chance to question you as closely?"

Venus inhaled a shaky breath. "I'll answer all your questions . . . if I can."

"Ambivalent but polite."

"You want true confessions?" she began acerbically. Then she shook her head, her body going lax. "I'm afraid this isn't going to work. I'd have better luck pleading with my landlady."

Cautiously, Eli observed her for a moment. Then he approached her and put his arms loosely around her. "You've had a rough time lately—losing your company, then this thing tonight. Forgive me for being so . . . forthright. I'll do better."

"So will I." Her breathing was impeded all at once, as though she'd just run a marathon race. The sudden fluttering shyness was an alien sensation. "I've read the papers, and I know you've had problems of your own. Being accused of undercutting the family business must have been a blow."

"It was." Eli's hands tightened fractionally at her back. "Why don't you unpack your things, shower if you like. I'll throw together an omelet."

"But it's late, nearly eleven o'clock. Did you forget dinner, too?"

"No, I've eaten. But I have a sudden appetite for more."

Venus stared at him, her skin prickling at the unconscious double entendre. Was it unconscious? The man should be registered with the police as a lethal weapon.

Eli Weldon-Tate was considered ruthless by some on the exchange. But everyone admired him for his cunning intellect and his superior strength. Eli Weldon-Tate was as tough as old boots.

She couldn't read anything behind that enigmatic smile. He was a shark in business. Was he the same with women? She had read about his exploits in the gossip columns, which labeled him a "dangerous but worthy investment."

Eli noticed the curious look on her face. "Are you planning my murder, Miss Wayne?" He stepped back and tapped her nose with his finger. "See you in a bit."

After a quick shower, Venus pulled on a fresh pair of jeans and a casual blouse. Then she headed toward the lower floor of the apartment.

One door to the left side of the corridor was ajar. Pushing it wide, Venus discovered a library with wall-to-wall books from ceiling to floor. An ornate, very large mahogany desk dominated the room with a light brown leather chair behind it. One wall had the business trades from around the world neatly draped over dowels.

Gravitating toward them, Venus reached out a hand. The *Wall Street Journal* featured an article on defunct investment companies. Teague and Wayne was mentioned. Venus felt the blood drain from her body as she perused the story, which mentioned Jeremy's death and the debts the company had accrued. A sharper pain knifed through her, taking her by surprise. Most of the sorrow she'd felt for Jeremy's death had given way to a cold, lonely numbness.

Eli had entered the room quietly. When he noticed the way her hands clenched the copy of the *Journal*, he hesitated. What article was she reading? he wondered, wanting to know all he could about the lovely Venus Wayne.

"You are welcome to use this room and all the research material at any time," he assured her, "but for now, you should eat."

Venus started slightly, then nodded and turned toward the door.

As she passed him, Eli noticed that her face was waxy white, as though she'd just read her own obituary. He was going to get to the bottom of this. Something was wrong in her world. Eli didn't know what the problem entailed, but he vowed to use all his power and strength to make it right.

Chapter Three

Venus was having problems adjusting to the subdued work environment on the top floor of the Weldon-Tate Building, but that was a piece of cake compared to living in Eli's apartment.

Teague and Wayne had always been hectic, and the messenger job was constant motion, but she'd handled them. There was no handling Eli Weldon-Tate. He was a hurricane in a three-piece suit, a cataclysmic force fitted with silk and finest worsted.

It was a paradox! He angered and confused her, but she was strangely happy with him. At times she felt netted and boated like a tuna, at other times there was such peace with him.

He was a joy to work with, his intellect and mastery of the business world challenging her constantly. She had never learned so much, never had her personal knowledge utilized to the limit. Yet when he was close to her, she felt threatened somehow, always out of breath. He used up all the oxygen.

Despite all her good intentions, she was still living in Eli's apartment. Every time she mentioned her search for a place to live, he insisted that she "stay for another week or so . . . until you're settled into your new position at Weldon-Tate."

When he had learned of her experience with Teague and Wayne, he immediately promoted her within his company. Venus's head spun when she remembered the way she'd been swiftly plucked from the mail room and given an office just down the hall from Eli. Although she'd expressed concern over her shaky reputation, Eli refused to pander to the opinions of others. "Your reputation is impeccable. All the accounts you handled at Teague and Wayne showed a profit. I refuse to let your keen instincts go to waste in the mail room!"

Her official title was special assistant to the CEO. Eli gave her a free hand with most of her projects, and she appreciated that. What frightened her witless was the feeling that life without Eli would be gray and one-dimensional. And the sensation grew every day. When had it begun?

The first days had been a baptism of fire, the skeptical glances of the top echelon staff following her each time she moved. Eventually, they had come to respect her, and the atmosphere was becoming comfortable.

Her first ally was Deena Liest, the receptionist for the penthouse office area. The cherubic-looking Deena was very popular with the others on the floor, and she had instantly warmed to Venus, making her feel welcome.

Bonnie, Eli's secretary, also befriended Venus. If she had been reticent the first days, she'd become increasingly friendly and was very helpful with any questions Venus had.

Of course, some of the faces at Weldon-Tate were familiar to Venus from her years on Wall Street. A few of the investment counselors were college acquaintances, while Venus recognized others from industry get-togethers. The company's corporate lawyer had been a close friend of Venus's partner. And although Venus had never been too crazy about Benedict James, it was nice to know that she had an ally—even if it was a sullen one.

There was so much to learn. Though her business background was sound, her self-confidence had been dented by the loss of her company.

In terms of her personal finances, Venus had never ridden the investment boom as hardily as her partner. Jeremy had pooh-poohed her wariness. "You'll never get anywhere if you don't take a few chances," he'd always said. He'd used risky trading strategies. And their firm had ended up with a corporate margin debt into the millions.

Because of Jeremy's death, the huge amount of debt had landed in Venus's lap. In a skittish market, Venus had been left with no choice but to dissolve their beloved company. The surviving-member clause in their insurance policy had helped some, but to clean up the debit, she'd had to use her savings, her car, stereo, and other assorted possessions. She was down to the bone fiscally, but she was nominally debt free, except for a few loans that she was making monthly payments on. No way to go but up!

Venus shook her head as the avalanche of memories washed over her. Most times she was able to fight them off, but at the moment they overwhelmed her. If only she could forget about the sniper and the ransacking of her apartment. Maybe one day she could put it all in perspective.

Many of the allegations that shrouded the reputation of her company weren't true. Fighting them was difficult. Didn't anyone listen to the truth anymore? More and more she wanted to confide her troubles to Eli, but she'd held back. If she ever broke down in front of him, she would never forgive herself. She had to be strong . . . keep moving ahead.

"Oh, Jeremy, what happened?" she asked aloud. Jeremy hadn't been available for his clients in the last days. This was brought up, time after time. Her lawyer wasn't too sure that there wouldn't always be a bit of a cloud over her name and reputation, but she intended to prove him wrong.

She shivered as she recalled the many confrontations she'd had with the clients of Teague and Wayne, over the phone and in person. How Jeremy's clients had distrusted her, vilified her when she had tried to talk with them. Jeremy had merely hung up on clients when they called. After his death she had taken the heat for his actions. Yet she missed her ebullient friend who, in her eyes, had been more foolish than malicious.

If only Jeremy hadn't died. If only he had confided in her more . . .

"Daydreaming?" Eli would have liked to pick her up and carry her out of there back to the apartment they shared. Damn the walls between them. They were always together, but at times they were worlds apart.

Blinking, Venus looked up at Eli, her breath catching at his nearness. He had leaned down close to her, and when she'd looked up, their mouths were just inches apart. "Uh, just thinking."

"Good. You have the mind for it. Incidentally I like that memo you wrote to Bonnie. You should have sent it directly to me." God, how he wanted to kiss her, not discuss business.

"Er, I thought I should go through Bonnie." His mouth looked wonderful.

"Thank you for thinking of company harmony,"

Eli told her dryly. "But next time you can come straight to me."

"All right."

"I'll leave you to your work. I'll be by to pick you up for lunch in half an hour." It relaxed him to know that she was in a nearby office, that by opening a door he could see her. Though there had been no repetition of the shooting, it made him edgy when she wasn't under his eye. Was he really any closer to her than that first night? "See you later, okay?"

Venus nodded. She enjoyed their lunches . . . and their dinners . . . and their breakfasts. But she wondered about the wisdom of spending so much time with this dynamic man.

She stared at the computer in front of her with Dow quotes dancing up the screen. Eli was kind to her. Why did she feel so threatened, so fenced? Being on her own so long had made her independent. She'd learned early to rely on herself, and she liked it that way. And now Eli was drawing her into his life, keeping her under lock and key. If she didn't like his protection, she could walk away . . . but why did the thought of that pain her so?

She was torn. There were times when she felt smothered in the rarefied air of the top floor. And she often yearned to get to the Street and duke it out with competitors the way she and Jeremy had done countless times.

Forcibly putting Eli out of her mind, she immersed herself in her work. As usual, it absorbed her, pulling her into the aura of business that fascinated her. She always lost track of time while engrossed in work.

"Ready to go?"

"What? Oh, Eli, I'm not through here and I do have to finish."

Eli looked at his watch. "All right. There's someone I should see downstairs for a moment. I'll meet you at the Pomegranate. Tell the maître d' you're at my table."

"Naturally. Otherwise they wouldn't let me in, would they?"

"No," Eli said dryly as he left her office.

"Steamroller," Venus muttered at the door, her eyes going back to the computer and pressing the print-out button. Again the work gripped her, and she lost track of time.

"Getting the latest Dow?"

"What?" Venus whirled around in her chair. "Oh, hello, Benedict. I'm afraid you just missed Eli. He already left for lunch."

Benedict James chuckled. "It's about time he left early. Pulling Eli away from work is like pulling teeth. Probably lunching with one of his cronies who'd rather live on his considerable annuities than put in a day's work."

Venus smiled. "Some people are more fortunate. Mint juleps, sandy beaches, and early retirement."

Benedict nodded. "Personally, I enjoy wrestling with business deals. How's your work going? Do you find the job interesting?"

"Very, but complex." Venus paused. Although Benedict had been a friend to her former partner, she'd always found him stiff and distant. "I know most people think Eli's crazy to have hired me, but—"

"Don't be silly. Eli is the boss, and he usually has pretty good judgment." Benedict's smile widened. "Besides, Jeremy always told me you had a good business head. That kind of praise gets around on Wall Street."

Venus could feel the blood rush to her face. The recognition pleased her. "I'm trying very hard to be useful, and I do have good credentials—"

"Yes, you do. Masters degree from the Maxwell School of Business, Syracuse University. I'm sure you'll work out, Venus. If there's any way I can help, call on me." He raised his brows at her sharp scrutiny. "Don't look so surprised that I know about your schooling. Jeremy filled me in on a lot of things. And Eli keeps very well documented dossiers on all his people."

"I see." Venus controlled an uneasy shiver with great effort. So Eli knew all about her, did he?

"I like to keep abreast of things, Venus," he said. "Will you tell Eli to call me?"

She nodded.

Removing the disks from her machine, she carefully filed them and locked the drawer. She had always been fussy with her records, but she was more so since the demise of her business.

Sighing, Venus tossed her shoulder bag over one arm and grabbed her winter coat. It was two weeks until Christmas and she still had a few loans to pay. She didn't have the money for a Christmas tree . . . but it could be worse. At least she had a roof over her head and a job.

Tonight she'd be with Eli, and that was more Christmas joy than she'd ever had. Her independent nature wouldn't let her be his houseguest for too long. She had to get back on her feet and start again, but it was wonderful to think of spending Christmas with him, to linger in his company, even if it couldn't be forever.

Taking the elevator to the street level, she forced

her mind to focus on other things as she made her way along the concourse to the Broadway exit. Outside, the shop windows were bursting with glitter and goodies.

It was when she paused in front of one of the shops that she noticed the man for the first time.

Maybe she wouldn't have noticed him if he hadn't been so incongruous in the well-dressed river of people. He looked like an unmade bed in his wrinkled dark suit and hat, his thick eyeglasses reflecting the holiday lights. He was medium height, burly, with a cigarette hanging from the side of his mouth. As her gaze touched him, Venus had the distinct impression that he deliberately looked away from her. Shrugging, she moved on and glanced at her watch. She had to hurry. She'd kept Eli waiting for almost a half hour, and the Pomegranate was still three blocks away.

When she paused for the light on Broadway, she felt a sudden push at her back. Gasping, she tried to maintain her balance, but the force was too strong. She catapulted forward—straight into the path of a speeding yellow cab. Somehow she was pulled back out of the line of traffic.

"Hey, lady, you okay? You gotta be careful, dashin' out like that." A workman was at her side, his face revealing his concern.

"Yes, thank you. Did you pull me back?" Venus looked around behind her and saw the burly man she'd seen in the concourse scurrying away. The dark-suited man with the slouch hat and spectacles!

"No, it wasn't me. I think it was that woman."

Venus looked in the direction the man was pointing and saw a large, tall woman in a fur coat moving rapidly away. "I wish I could have thanked her," Venus said.

"Naw, don't worry about it. New Yorkers help each other." The man grinned, showing a space where a tooth should have been. "You okay now? I gotta get goin'."

As Venus hurried along the avenue, she mulled her near-miss with the cab, the man she'd seen on the concourse, and the woman hurrying away.

Pushing open the door of the Pomegranate, she took a deep breath.

The maître d' materialized as she approached the main dining room. "May I help you?"

"It's all right, André. She's with me." Eli appeared behind the other man.

"Ah, very well, sir. This is the Miss Wayne you were expecting?"

"Yes," Eli said absently, staring at Venus, then moving closer, his arms going out to her.

She stared at him for a second, a strangled sigh rising in her throat as his strong arms enclosed her.

He led her to one side, where they were in the shelter of a huge, healthy palm tree. "What's wrong? You look pale. Are you ill? Shall I take you home?"

"I . . . fell into traffic. Some woman pulled me back in time, or I would have been hit by a cab." Shaken laughter mixed with a sob edged from her tight mouth.

"Dammit, I never should have left you to walk here alone!" Eli cuddled her close to him. "You should go home for the afternoon. I'll take you."

"No! I have reports to do."

Eli stared down at her for a moment, then he kissed her gently. "You're trembling. Let's get some soup into you." Keeping his arm around her, he led her through a maze of tables to a sheltered half-moon booth.

Other diners looked at him curiously, but Eli didn't seem to notice.

"I'm fine, really." Venus's knees began to shake the moment she was seated. "Do you see a black cloud hovering over my head?"

Her shaken smile jarred him more than her news. "Venus . . . tell me what really happened."

Numb, she watched as he signaled a waiter. What could she tell him? She didn't know anything.

"Get me some cognac. At once," Eli told the waiter.

"Cognac on an empty stomach will make me sick," Venus told him matter-of-factly as she threaded her fingers together.

"And bring the bouillabaisse—now," Eli commanded.

"You're very dictatorial." Venus smiled shakily.

"You've had a shock. And it could have been much worse." He felt ill all at once as he pictured her on the street, face down.

"Someone said that it was a woman who pulled me back in time," she said tiredly, the back of her head pressed to the banquette.

"You should have brought her with you." Eli lifted the snifter to her lips. "Take a sip. Your food will be here soon."

Venus managed one sip, but the second one made her gasp. "No more." She coughed. "The woman disappeared into the crowd." Like the bespectacled man. Was it paranoid to think she might have been pushed? Was she just jumping to conclusions because of all the things that had happened to her lately?

Venus shook her head, her eyes closing for a moment.

"Sorry. I don't mean to badger you." Eli slid closer, so that their bodies were touching.

Venus opened her eyes. "You weren't. I'm just so glad to be here." She lifted her left hand and gazed at her watch. "But I don't have long."

Eli took her wrist and kissed it, feeling the slight clamminess of her skin. "We have plenty of time." He stared at her. "Maybe I should take you to the hospital."

"No," she responded quietly without opening her eyes.

The waiter reappeared with a bowl of French chowder and placed it in front of her.

"Here." Eli lifted the spoon.

"I can feed myself," Venus told him, sitting straighter, smothering a wince as she felt a sudden soreness in her back.

Taking the spoon from him, she tasted the soup, pushing her fuzzy musings to the back of her brain.

"It's good, isn't it?" Eli asked her smoothly.

"Yes." She savored the richness of the stew in her throat.

"Have some more."

"I do feel better," she mused after she'd fortified herself with several spoonfuls. "I might even be ready to cross swords with you," she told him impishly.

"You do it all the time, Venus," he drawled.

"Is that why your eyes are flashing like train signals?"

Venus pushed back her empty bowl, relieved that some of the dizziness she'd experienced had receded. It had been a fearful moment, and it made her blood congeal to think of it. Later, when she was calmer, she would try to recall exactly what had happened.

Eli grinned, relief filling him. She was bouncing back. That was enough for him. "Would you like dessert, Venus? It might offset some of the acid in your disposition."

"Poor sport."

Eli leaned forward. "You're getting your color back, lady."

"The bouillabaisse did the trick."

"Would you like to spend the afternoon at an art auction? A friend of mine tells me there's a good one today."

Venus laughed. "Just like that. Walk away from the job?"

"Just like that."

"It sounds wonderful, and I would like to do it one day, but I should get my work done."

Eli smiled. "There's a great deal in Manhattan that I want to show you."

Venus felt her heart kick into overdrive. Eli was talking of the future. For so long her future had been shaky and uncertain. How wonderful it would be to have Eli in that picture.

He summoned the maître d'. "André, please get me a cab . . . and a phone." He looked back at Venus. "I'm going to take you to my physician."

"No! Please, I have a slight headache, nothing more, and I would really like to work."

"And I would feel better if a doctor looked at you."

André returned to the table with the phone and whispered to Eli.

"The cab's here. Indulge me." Eli smiled at her as he dialed. "Just let Will Doran look at you. It won't take a minute."

"There's no need," she said lamely. "The doctor is probably busy."

"Will? Eli. Could you do me a favor and look at a friend of mine now? Thanks. I owe you a lunch to make up for it."

In minutes they were out of the restaurant and into a cab heading uptown. Fifth Avenue looked wonderful, all dressed for Christmas. They sped down a cross street to Park Avenue, which also bore the lights and trimmings of the season.

"Here we are."

"This isn't necessary."

"It is," Eli told her, his smile tight.

Dr. Doran smiled at Venus. "Out, Eli. You don't run this office."

The examination was soon over and Venus had a clean bill of health.

She didn't speak to Eli until they were in a cab once more. "Thank you for being so concerned."

"I'm glad you're fine."

She smiled, but her eyes were guarded. Another door in the Eli Weldon-Tate trap was closing on her and she felt more hemmed in than ever. Yet ... being cherished was a great sensation. "I owe you a great deal."

"You owe me nothing," he said smoothly in a voice laced with steel.

"Don't protect me too much," she warned. "I'm my own woman."

"I didn't think I was doing that," Eli snapped.

"I want to stand on my own feet."

"Good for you."

"I don't mean to sound ungrateful—"

"I never asked for your gratitude."

Venus felt off track, out of sync. She and Eli could talk quietly to each other, and yet be warring. Was there ever such an anomaly as Eli Weldon-Tate? So hateful and lovable.

All at once Eli turned to her, moving closer. "We've endured many crises, Venus Wayne. Do you think the time is coming when we'll have a little quiet in our lives?"

Venus pictured them seated in front of a cozy fire, arms around each other. "Um, not if there's another Black Monday."

Eli took her hand and pulled it through his arm. "Don't dwell on the past. It's true that day has colored a great many of our moments since we met, but let's put it aside for the next hour. The sun is shining in Manhattan, Christmas is two weeks away, and we're in the most exciting city in the world." He pointed out the windows. "Look at the Cartier building."

Venus smiled at the huge red bow that wrapped around the turn-of-the-century building. As the cab continued down Fifth Avenue, they passed the spires of St. Patrick's Cathedral, the ice skaters at Rockefeller Center, and the festively dressed windows of Lord & Taylor. Venus felt as if she were seeing the city for the first time. "The whole world is lovelier at Christmas, isn't it?" she murmured.

"Yes," Eli answered, his voice low and hoarse. "Especially when seen at the side of a beautiful woman."

ChapterFour

Venus felt uneasy. She would never be able to explain to anyone, least of all herself, why she had been so intrigued by the account currently detailed on her computer screen. A week ago while doing some routine checks, she'd noticed a strange pattern in the Wade portfolio. Curious, Venus had researched the man's account, delving into past investments, losses and gains.

Now she wished she'd never done it. So much in the file seemed so familiar to her. Old wounds were opened as she stared at an investment portfolio that resembled some of the mishandled accounts she'd had to contend with when Jeremy died.

All those old sensations crowded in on her, carrying her back to her own debacle. In her pursuant investigation of the Wade file, one company's name had surfaced, again and again . . . Olympus.

That name had become all too familiar to her when she'd been fighting her way through the mountain of debt accrued by Teague and Wayne. Now here it was again in a prominent portfolio belonging to Weldon-Tate.

Who had Jeremy dealt with at Olympus?

Wasn't the company in some kind of trouble with the IRS? Venus remembered researching the firm but had found only a short blurb in one journal. No one had surfaced as the owner, though the search was on to find a culpable party.

Venus racked her brain, trying to recall what Jeremy had said about the people at Olympus. When she had told him that she didn't want to take her clients in that direction, he had never again mentioned the high-flying purchasing group.

She picked up her phone and dialed Reggie Leeds. An old friend from school, Reggie had drifted away in the past few months as he and Jeremy had struck sparks with each other. Jeremy had derided what he called Reggie's "cloying fiscal conservatism."

"Sure," Reggie told her. "I know a little about Olympus. Most people an the Street know 'a little' about them." There was a long pause.

"Why the reticence, Reg? Tell me what you're thinking."

"Well, the latest word is that Olympus had a great deal of help from Weldon-Tate."

Venus couldn't believe her ears. "What are you saying? Weldon-Tate is highly respected. Most of the clients who suffered have already been compensated . . . and very well, too."

"I'm just telling you what I've heard. And if the dry rot starts at the top and moves downward . . ."

Anger assailed her. "Reg, you are impugning a very well established company and—"

"Look, Venus, you called me. I'm only repeating the talk on the Street." Reggie paused. "You had your head in the sand with Jeremy. Don't get caught the same way twice."

The truth of his words cut her, wounding her conscience. "Are you sure about this?"

Reggie sighed. "As sure as anyone can be about

rumors on the Street. I'm pretty damn sure that Olympus is shaky. No one seems to be able to trace the corporate heads. But the latest rumors link Weldon-Tate with them."

It was the last thing Venus wanted to hear. Well, she couldn't kill the messenger just because the news was bad. "Thanks, Reggie."

"Hey, don't sound so glum, kid. It's been a long time. Let's have lunch one day."

"I'd love to get together, Reggie. Name a date." She laughed when he suggested the next day.

By the time she hung up the phone, Venus was smiling.

"Who's Reggie?"

Venus jumped and turned around to face a scowling Eli. "Don't do that. I nearly jumped out of my skin."

"You haven't answered my question."

"And I won't. You don't proctor my life." Venus noticed the angry gleam in Eli's eyes. She knew he was merely concerned for her safety. Nevertheless, she had a right to speak to her friends. "I'm grateful for—"

"I think we've had this fool conversation before," Eli growled. Before she could explain, he spun on his heel and returned to his office.

Later in the day, she knocked on the door of his office and leaned in. Eli was on the phone. He nodded to her once and went on with his conversation.

Venus dropped the revenue evaluations on his desk and turned away just as he replaced the receiver. She was at the door when his voice stopped her.

"My uncle is joining us for dinner this evening, Venus."

She breathed a sigh of relief at the relaxed tone in his voice, happy to put aside the strain that had been between them. "I can fend for myself, Eli. I wouldn't want to barge in on a family dinner if—"

"He wants to see you. He's been after me for days," he said.

"I see."

"Are you free?" Eli asked abruptly. When she nodded, he said, "Good." Then he picked up a portfolio in front of him as if he were dismissing her.

This tiptoeing around was beginning to drive Venus crazy. When she'd decided to stay at Eli's apartment, she'd vowed not to lose her independence. But day by day, she was slipping, succumbing to Eli's will, embracing his world.

Would she ever stand on her own two feet again? She hesitated for a moment, then turned and left his office.

That evening, Eli drove her home as usual. Tonight the warm aura that was usually surrounding them seemed to be missing. Their usual easy discussion of the day's events was strained. In the cloistered silence of the expensive auto, Venus wished she was in the subway. She felt imprisoned in the high-powered car.

When they finally pulled into the underground garage, Venus had the sensation of being smothered. Every indrawn breath was loud, cacophonous, seeming to shatter the uneasy silence.

Opening her door, she got out and hurried toward the elevator, taking deep, relieved breaths. As usual Eli had used up all the air. The intelligent, reasonable solution would be to flee—run from him, as far and fast as her legs would take her. She was an independent woman who could make it on her own. She should leave him. But why did that thought make her want to cry?

When she felt an arm around her waist, she stiffened.

"I'm sorry. I shouldn't have snapped at you in the office. I was a bear because I was jealous." Eli kissed the nape of her neck. "It's a new, damned unpleasant sensation for me."

"Jealous?" Breath rasped from her body, her heart slipping out of rhythm. "Of what?"

"There's a squeak in your voice. You sound like a little girl. Nervous?"

"Certainly . . . not." Venus took a deep breath, closing her eyes for an instant. "Reggie Leeds is a friend from school. I called him to get information about a strange company listed on several accounts in my firm and . . . on some of the Weldon-Tate portfolios. Venus exhaled. "And we're going to lunch tomorrow."

"I see. You didn't have to explain."

"I know that."

"We'd better get going. Uncle Dismas is punctual."

Venus stepped back from him, staring up into his eyes. "Eli, I want you to know, I've heard the rumors about you—insider trading, undercutting and the rest. I don't believe any of it." Venus was never more sure of anything in her life.

"Thank you. Have I told you that I love having you in my house?"

Venus smiled and nodded, despite the fact that she knew she would have to leave him soon. Although she dreaded setting up a new apartment, she was determined on the course.

Life without Eli was a gray prospect. The short time they'd been together had put a glow into her life, a warmth she'd never experienced. He was her candle in the darkness.

Even now, they moved as though of one accord, his arm at her waist.

Once in the elevator, he turned her to face him, his mouth touching hers, worrying her lips apart.

"Oh, Eli," Venus sighed. She was drowning and flying high in the air at the same time. The sensation was wild . . . and wonderful. Her hands had a life of their own as they reached up and clasped Eli behind the neck.

"You're beautiful," he muttered against her mouth, his voice thick and uneven.

Venus didn't open her eyes. She didn't want the moment to end. Eli Weldon-Tate was sexy, alive, and wonderful. He filled all the voids in her life, painted out the black spots with a blinding white. It scared her how much she wanted him, needed him . . .

Her eyes snapped open and she looked right into his.

"What is it, Venus? Tell me."

She shook her head.

"Do you know how much I want you?" His voice was husky with passion.

"I have a few wants myself."

Eli kissed her again, holding her pliant body tightly.

Passion, like a live, hot wire coiled around them, burning the atmosphere, creating an aura just for them.

A hundred good reasons for freeing herself filtered through Venus's mind and dissipated. Reality was Eli. Strong, tall, and wonderful, Eli with the electric green eyes and the hard body that now burned against hers in fiery need.

The electricity between them made Venus reel. Never in her life had she imagined the erotic response that coursed her body now. The raw desire was a new flame, blazing over her, stunning her.

Her beauty filled him like an incredible incense. Never had a woman been so overwhelming. When he held her in his arms, the world receded and left only Venus in his sight.

Eli had a hazy knowledge that the elevator doors had opened into the penthouse, but he didn't release her. Her body had magnetized him, welded him to her, and he didn't want to be free.

"Eli? Getting a massage? Or giving one?" The old man's gravelly voice penetrated the private world they had created in the elevator.

Eli lifted his head a fraction, glancing toward the sardonic voice. "Uncle Dismas. Nice to see you."

"Really? Then why do I feel like a fifth wheel? I'm sure you wish I were in Pittsburgh. Extract yourself from the girl and introduce us."

Red-faced, Venus tried to struggle free.

But Eli kept her close to him, allowing her to turn slightly so that he could do the honors. "We had a tiff and were making up."

"Is that so?" Dismas narrowed his eyes for a better look. "The Versailles Treaty wasn't as involved," he observed. "No wonder the gal is out of breath. How do you do? I'm Dismas Weldon."

Still flustered, Venus stammered, "I'm—I'm—" For a moment Venus was blank.

"Alice in Wonderland? Little Red Riding Hood?"

"Uncle!" Eli stared at the older man, who shrugged benignly. "This is Venus Wayne."

"Bright thing, isn't she. Does she often forget her name?"

"Only in the company of crusty curmudgeons," Venus said, finally finding her voice. Damn Eli Weldon-Tate—and all his relations! Her legs felt like rubber and she had double vision. Eli was bad for her health.

Eli laughed and led her into the foyer. "Venus doesn't scare easily, Uncle."

"And it would seem only you render her mute, Eli."

"Uncle!" A grimace replaced Eli's smile.

Venus looked into the man's flashing eyes, so like his nephew's, and bit back a retort when she noted how much fun Dismas Weldon was having.

"You should have been a model, Miss Wayne, not a business analyst. Even though Eli says you're quite good."

"I am."

"I meant in business."

"So did I," Venus shot back.

Dismas looked pleased with himself, his mouth twitching as he fought back a smile. Then he turned away, moving down the hall. "I told Monihan that dinner would be at seven," he called over his shoulder before he disappeared into the library.

"Auspicious beginning." Eli turned to Venus, chuckling when she shook her head. "Don't get mad at me." He reached out a finger to caress her lower lip. "Damn Uncle Dismas for interrupting us."

Unable to say anything, Venus merely stared at him.

Eli kissed her once, very hard, then strode toward the stairs, taking them two at a time. Halfway up he looked back at her. "Better hurry. It's nearing seven."

Venus climbed the stairs more slowly. The rat! A fine way to meet his uncle, caught like a teenager in the backseat of a Chevy!

As she washed and dressed at top speed, her

mind reviewed the kiss in the elevator. In those few moments her life had turned upside-down and sideways. It was scary. Eli had explored places in her heart that had been previously unknown to her. Her response to him shocked her.

The prospect of facing Dismas Weldon across a dinner table gave her goose bumps. Even in the short introduction to him she had noted the sharp scrutiny, the intelligent quirk to that strong mouth. Did he realize how deeply shaken she'd been by his nephew's kiss? She didn't want to deal with that. It was hard enough to face Eli without Dismas Weldon looking at her knowingly. Although he was slight of build, he was no lightweight in the brains department. More than once in her short professional life she'd met men of similar mettle—tough and intelligent, able to accurately assess a situation, the business aggression masked behind a serenity that couldn't quite hide the determination and purpose.

Dismas Weldon didn't miss a trick. He would immediately see that she had fallen prey to Eli's charms.

Venus gave a final tug to the coral-hued beaded mini that she'd found in a Third Avenue boutique. She'd once made some great buys on designer clothes, but not even thrift shops drew her now, she thought ruefully as she turned in front of the mirror. Maybe the dress was a bit on the short side.

The silky, beaded material clung to her form, delineating every curve. Her legs were emphasized by the French-heeled pumps in the same hue as the dress. The dress and shoes had come as a set, and at the time she had considered them quite a bargain.

"Chin up," Venus instructed her reflection. Then she took a deep breath, opened her door, and stopped dead. "You!"

"You were expecting someone else?" Eli's eyes fixed on her, moving over her from her eyebrows to her toes. "Venus, you look beautiful."

"Thank you."

Eli frowned. "I'm not sure I want even my uncle to see you in that dress. So sensuous and lovely."

Her knees were melting again. The midnight-green cable-knit sweater deepened the color of his eyes. Was a man supposed to be beautiful?

"Kiss me, Venus." Eli placed his hands above her head on either side of the doorjamb, leaning close but not touching her.

Venus knew she should avoid him. Instead she extended one hand and cupped his freshly shaven jaw, her fingers smoothing over it, seeking greater knowledge of him. Leaning up, she nipped him on the chin, her fingers following to massage there. Then she moved closer, still on tiptoe, and bit his ear.

"If you're trying to tease me, it's working," he told her huskily.

"Just playing games."

"I play to win."

"So do I."

His dark, steely gaze assured her that he meant every word.

Eli's arm dropped around her waist, pulling her closer. "Why are you blushing?"

"I've been blushing since the day I met you."

Eli's mouth closed over hers in a deep, satisfying kiss that went on and on, until his chest was heaving in emotional response. His hands traveled over the beaded dress in restless quest.

Her body came to life at his touch. Venus felt beautiful. Were her eyes sparkling at that moment? Her skin must be luminescent, glowing. She had become new. Had her hair thickened and become more lustrous? Eli had a power that both awed and intrigued her. She wanted him desperately.

"Hey, you two, should I get Monihan to hose you down?" Dismas Weldon stood below them in the foyer, smiling gleefully.

"Damn my uncle," Eli muttered against her lips.

"It's okay," Venus said with a shrug as she slipped out of his embrace. "Besides, I'm hungry."

"So am I, but not for a damned dinner." Eli grinned ruefully and moved back a fraction. "Has anyone told you that you have a stevedore's appetite?"

"Years of grabbing meals while I honed my talents."

Eli watched her face tense slightly, as though she'd just told him too much. In many ways Venus Wayne was mysterious. It wasn't just her beauty that intrigued him. "Shall we go down and face the 'crusty curmudgeon'?"

Venus closed her eyes for a moment. "Don't remind me. I was a bit rude to your uncle, wasn't I?"

"Don't worry." Eli chuckled and kissed her ear. "He likes spunky women as much as I do. Let's go."

They descended the stairs hand in hand. The moment they walked into the spacious dining room, the butler came through from the kitchen.

"Has our dinner grown cold, Monihan?" Dismas inquired gently.

Venus looked at Eli's uncle and caught the expectant gleam in his eyes before it was quickly masked. A reluctant smile touched her mouth. "Troublemaker," she murmured.

Dismas scrutinized Venus, then burst into hearty laughter. "You don't stampede easily, girl. Now, sit down and tell me about your near miss with the taxi the other day."

In the act of shaking out his napkin, Eli stared at his uncle. "Who told you about that? I didn't."

"No? Maybe I heard it around the office."

"I'm perfectly fine, sir. A bruise or two, no more."

"I understand a woman pulled you to safety."

"I believe so, but I couldn't really see who helped me. The woman left the area in such a hurry, I wasn't able to thank her, either."

"Why the frown, Venus?" Eli hitched his chair closer to hers.

"I was just thinking about a strange man who was also there. He looked like a caricature of a Russian spy," she said, half laughing. "You know what I mean—dark hat and suit, with black-rimmed spectacles, stolid features, blocky build . . ." Her voice trailed off.

"He made an impression on you," Eli said slowly.

"Yes. I thought I saw him again the other day when I was looking in a shop window, but when I turned around he was gone."

"Imagination working overtime, you think?" Dismas asked nonchalantly.

"I suppose that could be it." Venus had the sensation that Dismas was not as insouciant as he sounded.

"Venus is very observant," Eli said, scowling at his relative.

The muted strains of a violin concerto emanating from the ceiling speaker was the only sound in the room for an instant. Then Dismas said good-naturedly, "Ah, here we are. Monihan has made some of his famous New England clam chowder."

"At your order, Uncle?"

"Well, I did phone him this morning." He glanced at Venus. "Curmudgeons do that."

"That's probably the nicest epithet ever applied to you," Venus retorted, fighting the rush of blood up her face.

Monihan snorted and Eli laughed.

Dismas shook his head. "She's got grit, Monihan."

"That she has, sir. Reminds me of you, she does."

"Ah, is that why I'm so drawn to her?" Dismas mused, his smile widening. "Maybe it's because I like to see my nephew dance to a lively tune."

"There is that, of course," Monihan murmured, unable to stifle the grin that creased his face.

"Don't you have a salad to toss, or something?" Eli glared at his butler, who stared back at him.

"No, I've made a marinated salad," Monihan answered, then turned on his heel and sauntered from the room.

"Smart aleck. I should fire him." Eli spoke to the swinging door that closed at the butler's back.

"Fat chance." Dismas touched Venus's arm. "Eli's in a temper. He would like you all to himself, with Monihan and me at the Devil's Door. Too bad for him, eh?"

Venus laughed in spite of herself as Eli glowered and his uncle beamed. "You'd start a fight in an empty house, as my Grandmother Wayne used to say."

"There's a shadow in your eyes," Dismas remarked. "Your grandmother must have been dear to you."

"She raised me," Venus said abruptly, concentrating on her hands clasped in her lap. "She loved me."

How had the lovely, vulnerable Venus Wayne ended up so alone in the world? Eli stared at her bent head for long moments.

"And how is Weldon-Tate holding up, my boy?"

"There's some thin ice, Uncle, and a few persons have looked askance at our merger with B. E. Hayson. Some view it as a hostile takeover, I hear."

"That's irrational and uninformed thinking, and you know it. Weldon-Tate rescued Hayson and the good heads on Wall Street realize that. Olympus would have eaten it alive and thrown the staff into the street." Dismas paused, steepling his hands. "But I do know you've made some powerful enemies with the takeover, Eli. I've been hearing rumors of discontent these past weeks. Watch your back, my boy."

Eli nodded. "I've picked up the same vibrations, Uncle. Don't worry, I've learned to be careful." Eli stared hard-eyed at the wineglass he cupped in both hands. "It would help if I knew all my enemies."

"True. It's times like these that I miss Benedict's father. He was very astute in dealing with companies like Olympus." Dismas looked thoughtful. "I still find it hard to believe he killed himself. Never knew a fellow with more joie de vivre . . . and intelligence to boot." Dismas shook his head. "Benedict has had big shoes to fill."

Eli nodded, his glance sliding toward Venus, catching her eye. His heart turned over when she smiled at him.

Dismas sipped more wine, his face thoughtful. "It would seem that Olympus counted highly on obtaining Hayson."

Eli shot a sharp look at his uncle.

But Venus's interest was piqued. "Who is the CEO at Olympus?"

Both men appeared to be startled.

"A man by the name of Glenn Boll is the titular

head," Dismas answered slowly, his eyes narrowing. "But he's been ill for some time now. I imagine that the board is running most things with an executive vice actually managing." Dismas steepled his hands. "Offhand, I can't think of who that might be. A great deal of money was funneled through Olympus before the crash. It would seem their losses would have to be in the mega figures, but there's no sign of flagging. Many of their clients took a drubbing, from what I hear."

"Why do you ask, Venus?" Eli noticed that she chewed at her bottom lip.

She shrugged. "The group intrigues me." She took a deep breath and faced Dismas squarely, her steaming chowder forgotten. "You see, sir, the company that my partner and I started has been dissolved. Many of the clients who went down hard also had accounts at Olympus. Coincidence, I suppose."

Eli placed his spoon next to his empty bowl. "No doubt. But there is a parallel with Weldon-Tate there. We also had clients who dealt with Olympus. Have you been researching this, Venus?"

Eli's question was innocuous, but all at once Venus felt as though a firecracker had been dropped into the middle of the room. "What is it? What's wrong?"

"Nothing. I just wondered if, perhaps, you'd done a comparison between your company and another . . . such as Weldon-Tate."

Venus shook her head, feeling every nerve on her body tingle. Why was Eli so furious? Did Weldon-Tate have something to hide?

During the short time she'd lived in this house, Venus had learned a great deal about the CEO at Weldon-Tate. Though Eli smiled and seemed very open and congenial, under the surface there were diamond facets that showed now and then—cold, hard edges that could cut through anything. It was a potent, dangerous side of him that she was sure most people never saw.

Dismas picked up a silver bell in the middle of the table and rang it peremptorily. "Time for the salad."

The electricity generated by the discussion of Olympus seemed to sizzle throughout the evening. Venus's body still crackled with intrigue, which went round and round her head for the rest of the meal. Dismas Weldon and his nephew knew something about Olympus and they didn't want to share it with her. And she'd also noticed Dismas's peculiar reaction when she'd spoken of the bespectacled man.

After dinner they moved from the dining room to the living room, where Monihan served exotic tea, tiny squares of short bread, Stilton cheese, and grapes.

Dismas didn't stay long after he had his coffee and cheese. "Monihan, you outdid yourself again. Like to change your mind and come work for me?"

"Ah, Mr. Weldon, you tempt a man. It wouldn't be that bad, I'm thinkin'." Monihan grinned when Eli turned in his chair to look at him.

"Have a brandy, Uncle?"

"You're wishing me in Pittsburgh again, Eli. Don't pretend."

"A short brandy, then." Eli had risen to his feet. "Uncle, when will you stop trying to steal my butler?"

"Never. Someday I'll succeed. Besides, that's not why you want me out of here." His glance slid toward Venus before he preceded the two of them out of the room. Dismas's gravelly voice echoed in the two-story foyer. "Good night, my dear. I look forward to the time when you dine in my home. And I hope it will be soon." He touched her hand for a moment.

"Thank you, sir."

"Take care of yourself, child. We're in a very tough business." His twinkling smile faded for a moment, then he stepped into the elevator and pressed the button.

In the sudden silence Eli pulled Venus toward him. "You could use some of that brandy I mentioned."

"I'm not much of a drinker," she whispered. Eli was more than enough intoxication for her. Whether he was with her or not, he was always at the forefront of her mind.

"This is a prescription for nerves, nothing more."

Venus faced him, feeling relaxed, warm, secure. "Why would your uncle tell me to take care of myself, Eli? Doesn't he trust women in business?"

"Uncle Dismas is not only intelligent, he's also a world-class feminist. He wouldn't be worried about having a woman in the firm." Eli glanced at the elevator doors that had closed behind his uncle, his eyes narrowing for a moment, then he turned to smile at her. "About that medicinal brandy."

"Now you're a doctor as well as a business entrepreneur?"

"Yes." Eli kissed her forehead. He sensed her unease. "What is it? Are you suddenly wary of being alone with me?"

Venus shook her head. "It isn't that."

"What, then?"

"I'm not sure you'll understand." Venus moved ahead of him into the living room.

"You look very sexy tonight," Eli said at her back.

Venus whirled to face him, her hands, palm outward, keeping a space between them. "Eli, listen to me. I called up a personal account today because it seemed to have many similarities to some of the accounts that my firm had handled."

"So? And were they the ones that went under in October?"

Lips parted, Venus nodded. "How did you know?"

"Because I can't see you pulling a file that's not part of your sector unless it had to with the failures of your business," Eli said smoothly.

"That makes sense," Venus answered slowly. He was holding something back.

"You just shivered. Are you cold?" Eli reached for her, pulling her into her arms. "Let's put business on the back burner now, shall we? We talked shop all through dinner. That's enough." With his face pressed to her hair he inhaled the lovely, elusive scent of her.

"And you're not angry with me for calling up that file?"

"No, not angry, but I do think you'd do better to concentrate on your own sector. There are certain accounts that I'm handling personally and they will come about, I'll see to that."

"But some of the accounts involved with Olympus—"

"Shh, business is over for today." Eli kissed her hair.

"Then I should go to bed," she ventured weakly.

"Umm, me, too." He tightened his hold on her, his mouth caressing the outer curve of her ear. "Your skin is satin."

"Thank you."

"There's that squeak in your voice again. Do you know I want you, Venus?"

"I have an inkling."

"Do you want me?"

"Eli, this is crazy." She leaned back from him, then closed her eyes and groaned when he pressed his mouth to hers in a feathery kiss.

"You call the shots all the way," he assured her. "If you don't want me to kiss you, tell me."

She didn't know if she could say the words that would send him away. "I . . . don't . . ."

"Yes?"

"I . . ."

"I'm listening."

"And I'm trying," Venus told him crossly, her mouth inches from his. "Damn you, you intrigue me, but don't read anything into that." Venus threaded her hands in his hair. "This isn't sensible," she muttered, wondering if there had been a man created since the dawn of time that could approximate Eli Weldon-Tate. He was so very special.

His mouth slid down her cheek. "Did I tell you I think red hair and violet eyes are totally incongruous and beautiful."

"Uh-uh." Venus was whirling in a kaleidoscopic vortex.

"I do."

"Sounds like a vow."

Eli leaned back from her. "Don't smirk, I might be making one."

"Don't go too fast. Both our lives are in turmoil right now, Eli."

"Venus, tell me you want me."

"I thought you wanted me to have brandy." She nuzzled her face against his neck. Insanity! She should stop this now before it was too late. Her blood was surging, roaring in her ears. Was she hearing the crash of her bridges collapsing behind her?

"I have some very fine cognac in my upstairs study." Eli kissed her cheek. "When you breathe into my neck that way, you send my pulse on a rocket ride." Eli lifted her into his arms and carried her easily up the stairs. At the top, he looked down at her, hesitating for a moment, then strode across the hall to his suite.

"I haven't seen your room." Venus was fearful but excited. She wanted Eli with an urgent, earthy need, but she was afraid of losing a part of herself.

"You wouldn't let me show it to you."

"Self-defense."

"Coward." Eli kicked open the door. "Well? Do you like it?"

Venus slid down his body, one hand coming up to cover her mouth, but she couldn't quite mask the mirth that welled up inside her.

"Venus!" Eli frowned down at her.

"It's a seduction scene. Coral and lime! Wow, Mr. Weldon-Tate, sir. A few beaded drapes would add the finishing touch."

Eli grimaced. "You do have a way of throwing cold water on things. Must you always cool me down?"

"That was not my intention," she told him soberly. "It's just that the color scheme is—is—unfortunate."

"Brat." Eli leaned down and tweaked her nose. "I didn't see it that way . . . until now."

"Sorry, Eli. It's just my opinion."

"I don't want you to hide your opinions from me. I want openness between us."

"But not blunt discourtesy. I should have kept my thoughts to myself. One day I'll learn to control my bizarre sense of humor and watch my mouth."

"I love your mouth." Eli bent to kiss her lips. "And I'm not as cooled down as I thought."

Venus chuckled deep in her throat. "Good." The feathery sensation of his lips was very erotic.

"I'll redecorate after Christmas."

"Don't! Please. The colors are . . . vibrant, and you like it."

"Maybe we can find some colors we both like." He let his hand lightly move down her arm. "We have Yule presents to think about, don't we?"

She nodded, pulling back from him just a tad. "Do you trim your own tree?"

Eli shook his head. "I usually have a department store deliver a decorated tree. I can see that wouldn't do for you. Shall we choose one? Buy the lights and decorations ourselves?" Her eyes glinted purple in the dim light of the room, warming him like a caress.

"Please. I love Christmas."

"I think I'm going to like this one myself. And I can't wait to show you off at the company Christmas party."

Venus smiled. "Sometimes you sound so possessive."

"I am, when it comes to you. Now, can we table the discussion?"

"Like the business discussion?" Why didn't she feel more hesitant with Eli? The one sexual relationship she'd had in college had been a short, painful one. The guy's macho attitude had been a complete turnoff. All her romantic feelings had dissipated after their first time together. Since then,

Venus hadn't desired another intimate relationship. She'd even wondered at times if something was wrong with her. But Eli had chased those fears away. In his arms, she was on fire.

"Will you please stop chattering and kiss me?" he teased.

"Well, if you insist." Venus pressed closer, feeling bold. It was the Christmas season. Why should she deny herself this gift? It might be her only one. She wanted Eli. Taking a deep breath, she pressed her mouth to his, her tongue touching his in a sensuous rhythm.

In seconds the world turned molten. Her emotions were lava, burning, spilling, igniting every pore of her body, until she was engulfed.

Eli placed her on the bed, then he followed her down, his hold on her never lessening.

Venus never knew how her dress slipped to the floor, but she was so grateful. She could feel the hard satin of Eli's skin against hers, and no sensation had ever given her such joy.

Body to body, they held each other, motionless. If they moved, the wonder would dissipate; their togetherness would dissolve.

"I want you, Venus . . . I need you." The lacing of surprise in his voice escaped Venus because she, too, was caught in the deluge of passion that had overtaken them.

"Love me, love me." All the reservations she'd had about making love evaporated in the sweeping heat of Eli's embrace. No man had ever called forth such a response from her.

"Easy, love, not so fast," he said huskily, a tremor in his voice.

"Too late, I want you too much." She smiled when she heard his chuckle against her skin.

He leaned up on one elbow, studying her. "You have skin like the purest cream . . . your body is so slender and curvy . . ." Eli bent his head, his mouth moving slowly down her form, kissing her breasts, caressing her abdomen, making her stomach muscles clench in delight.

He slid down her body until his tongue was flicking over her instep.

"Eli!" Her voice was ragged, her breathing uneven as she reacted to his lovemaking. Never in her life had she envisioned a man worshiping her body in such a way. Venus was stunned by the rivers of joy that coursed through her.

"I'm here, darling. I want to make you happy."

Venus's head twisted and turned on the bed as rapture filled her. Colors exploded behind her eyes. Stars and planets soared around her.

Eli was a man who never lost control, no matter how hot his desire. He was always in charge—until now. Inch by inch, pore by pore Venus Wayne was pulling him apart and rebuilding him. Passion surged through him, emotion throbbing in every vein. A need to cherish her drove his every move. Giving her pleasure and satisfaction became his mission.

When his tongue intruded in the most elemental way, Venus's body arched like a bow. Nothing had prepared her for the fire that threatened to consume her, that burned her skin with the cool silkiness of love. Hot or cold? What was she? Her body was leaden with love. Yet she flew like an arrow to the sun.

Was this the wonder of lovemaking? These feelings were new, wondrous. There were love ballads all around them, and the lyrics were clear. Venus belonged to Eli!

Bodies moist with the mist of passion, they climbed the elemental mountain, clasped in each other's arms. In one cataclysmic moment they surged together, discovering the cosmos where only lovers go.

Eli had never known such a fever. And he felt humbled and exalted to know that Venus shared the same ecstasy. That had shaken him to his soul.

Venus felt tears on her cheeks, but she didn't open her eyes. She wanted to hold the moment forever.

Mute and loving, they held each other and fell asleep.

Later that night Eli awoke and looked down at the woman in his arms. Tenderness suffused him as he kissed her. In slow wonder, he felt her response, though her eyes were still closed. His body hardened in an almost instant reaction.

"It's so wonderful with you, Venus."

"I never knew." She opened her eyes, her arms coming up to clasp him. Long, slow moments with Eli had taught her so much. As his arms tightened around her, Venus grew bolder with every stroke. Her body was soon eager, ready.

Air rasped from her lungs as, finally, Eli pulled her under him, his gentle entry smooth and strong. When he heard her cry out, he hesitated. "Venus?"

"Love me, Eli, love me."

"Forever, darling."

Chapter Five

The next day Venus rose from the bed before Eli, who slumbered deeply.

They'd made love many times in the night, and each time Venus was ready and eager. Never in her life had she expected to give such a deep, earth-shattering response. All her preconceived notions about love being a painful, rough experience had been washed away by Eli's tender touch. In one gentle, wonderful night, Venus had discovered love. She was in awe.

Showering and changing quickly in her own suite, she left him a note and went downstairs.

"You'll be having breakfast, miss?"

"Not this morning, Monihan. I just want to get moving."

"It's thin as a rail you are, and I'll not be picking you up when you drop over." The scowl almost masked the concern in the Irish butler's eyes.

"I'll be fine."

Venus took the bus and then walked crosstown to the office. Not once had she considered taking the car that Eli had told her was at her disposal. Pride wasn't the only thing holding her back. The car was a Rolls-Royce, and the thought of maneuvering it through Manhattan traffic made her stomach flip-flop.

It was snowing in Manhattan, and the buildings glittered like fairy-tale castles. The light dusting of snow covered the streets like the sugary icing on Christmas cookies. Venus inhaled deep breaths of air, trying to concentrate on the beauty of a New York Christmas, but all she could think of was how wonderful she had felt in Eli's arms. Never in her wildest dreams had she envisioned the joy that making love with him had brought her. Damn Eli Weldon-Tate! He had made her love him.

At the wide, polished doors of the Weldon-Tate Building she decided to buy a paper. Stopping and turning suddenly, she bumped into a woman. While she was apologizing, Venus caught sight of the bespectacled man on the other side of the kiosk. Then he was gone.

Cautiously, Venus paid for the paper and looked around again, but there was no one. By the time she reached the elevator she was almost able to convince herself that it had been her imagination.

Immersing herself in her accounts, Venus put the bespectacled man from her mind. But nothing would drive away thoughts of Eli and their night together.

Every year Weldon-Tate Enterprises threw a sumptuous Christmas party for its employees. Although Venus had been looking forward to the special event, she was taken aback by the lavish decorations adorning the ballroom of the Ritz Hotel. Full evergreens bedecked with candy canes and silver bows created a path leading to the parquet dance floor. And each banquet table bore a crisp snowy white tablecloth, silver votive candles, and a bouquet of white orchids and holly.

"It's a winter wonderland," Venus exclaimed, giving Eli's arm a squeeze.

He seemed surprised at her enthusiasm. "This?" His gaze combed the ballroom, as if he just noticed the festive sights and the rich scent of pine and cinnamon. "You're right. It is quite lovely," he said as he escorted her to their table. "But not as beautiful as you."

Venus had worn a shoulderless velvet gown with a bodice that hugged her delicate curves. The dark dress made her fiery red hair burst with warm color. The mere sight of her made Eli's muscles tighten with desire.

"If I had my way, I'd never leave your side through the entire evening," he whispered for her ears only. "But ... duty calls. We'll both have to mingle."

Even as Eli spoke, a board member was making his way to their table. With a reluctant glance, Eli murmured, "Will you save the last dance for me, Venus?"

Her eyes were an explosion of violet as she smiled at him. "Of course," she teased. "Anything for the CEO!"

As Eli became engrossed in conversation with his colleagues, Venus spent some time with her new associates. She found Deena Liest sipping a glass of wine beside a huge evergreen wreath illuminated by tiny red and white lights.

"Watch old Mr. Dismas." Deena nodded in the direction of Eli's uncle. "I swear, he's purposely waiting under that mistletoe, hoping to snare some unsuspecting female!"

Both women laughed, then Deena went on to relate humorous anecdotes about previous Weldon-Tate bashes.

Amid the delights of gourmet foods, fine wines, and spicy conversation, the evening passed quickly. After dinner Venus took to the dance floor with various eager partners. Although she was never far from Eli's watchful eye, his business associates kept him busy.

"Care to dance?" The familiar voice made Venus a bit uncomfortable. She slowly turned to face Benedict James, who smiled stiffly and offered his arm.

"I'd love to," Venus lied, avoiding his eyes as she walked toward the dance floor.

She had never understood Jeremy's friendship with this man. Somber and morose, Benedict James had always struck her as a bit of an oddball. There was something in his eyes—a strange look, like a drinking glass shattered beyond repair—that made her pity him. She knew he'd lost his father fairly recently, and he'd been saddened over Jeremy's death. But try as she might, Venus could never muster up feelings of compassion for Weldon-Tate's corporate attorney.

Forcing herself to smile at him, Venus couldn't shake the chills she felt in his arms.

And Benedict noticed. "Is my technique that bad, Venus?"

She shook her head, feeling instantly ashamed. "I guess I've just grown accustomed to Eli's style," she explained.

"Oh?" Benedict's eyes narrowed. "I'd be careful if I were you. You know, it can be dangerous to get too close to a man like Eli. A man at the top of a corporation has a lot of . . . secrets, entanglements."

A stab of fear shot through Venus, but she tried to maintain her composure. "Don't we all have secrets, Benedict?"

"Some of us more than others." He swung her through a turn so quickly, she had to struggle to keep her balance. "I'm telling you this for your own good. Watch your step with Eli. You've taken one fall, Venus. I'm sure you don't want to dirty your hands again."

Although Venus was breathless, there was no mistaking the menace in Benedict's voice. "You can't be serious," she gasped. "Eli's reputation is clean as a whistle. You're the one conducting the investigation to clear him! We both know he's honest to the core. Is there a snag in the investigation? Something I can help you with?"

Benedict held her uncomfortably close. "As far as I'm concerned, you already know too much. According to the firm's log book, you've been checking out files on Olympus. Does the Wade portfolio ring a bell, Venus?"

She nodded. "I know it's privileged information, but I've kept all that material under wraps."

His dark eyes were probing. "And have you asked Eli about his involvement with Olympus?"

"Yes—well, no, not in so many words. We talked about the company, but no one seems to have a grip on the—"

"Watch your step." Benedict stared into her eyes, then released her abruptly as the music stopped. "Stop poking around in matters that don't concern you. I'm afraid that Mr. Eli Weldon-Tate is one of those matters."

Riddled with confusion, Venus merely stepped back and folded her arms.

When she didn't answer, Benedict murmured, "Things aren't always what they seem, Venus. A pretty little thing like you should know that by now. Don't get caught in the next crash." Before she could respond, he strode away, disappearing amid the forest of glittering Christmas trees and chattering guests.

"You seem rather preoccupied." Eli's voice interrupted Venus's troubled thoughts.

"Just tired, I guess." She was shivering, despite the toasty warmth inside Eli's Rolls-Royce. The Christmas party had been festive and fun until her dance with Benedict put a damper on the evening.

As Eli concentrated on Manhattan traffic, she studied the smooth planes of his face. It seemed like a noble face, the face of an honest, trustworthy man. But could she really be sure?

"Benedict James was in an odd mood tonight," she said, carefully monitoring Eli's reaction.

He didn't flinch. "Oh, really?"

"He's annoyed at me for looking into Olympus's dealings."

Eli still didn't seem concerned.

"Did he mention anything to you?" Venus asked.

"No. Sounds like a typical reaction from Benedict, though. The man likes to be in control"—Eli looked over at Venus—"as we all do," he admitted.

"This seemed like more than a power struggle," she explained. "I mean, he kind of warned me to keep my nose clean—or else."

Eli shrugged. "Not an unusual piece of advice, coming from a corporate attorney. Don't worry about it." He reached over and gave her knee an affectionate squeeze. "Benedict's a good guy. His family's law firm has represented Weldon-Tate for years. He's one of the few men in this world that I trust."

Turning up the collar of her coat, Venus stared up at the man she so desperately wanted to love. *I hope you're right*, she thought. *And I hope to God that I can trust you!*

That night, their lovemaking took on a new, desperate tone. The gloom and doom forecast by Benedict James hung over Venus like a black cloud. Suddenly aware that her relationship with Eli wasn't necessarily a forever thing, she clung to him as if he were her beacon in a storm.

Tomorrow she might discover that he was a crook. Tomorrow she might uncover files linking *him* to Olympus and all the underhanded dealings that gave Wall Street a bad name.

Tomorrow she might discover evil, ruthless dealings, crimes so heinous that they could nearly justify the sniper attack in the lobby of his building.

But tonight he was hers. Her knight in shining armor, her golden savior. Deep in her heart, she couldn't believe that Eli had a bad bone in his body.

With that in mind, she have herself up to his strong embrace, his hot kisses, and the passionate, soulful rhythm of a love that defied reality.

At least for tonight.

"You are an early bird."

Startled, Venus looked away from the computer monitor. She hoped Eli wouldn't notice the information on the screen, part of her urgent attempt to get to the bottom of things. Haunted by fears and suspicions, she'd crept out of bed before dawn and taken a cab to the office.

Framed by the doorway, Eli looked like a suave model for a corporate fashion magazine. His tailored wool suit fit him like a glove, and his emerald-green tie brought out the intense highlights in his eyes.

"I missed you this morning," he said, approaching her like a stalking lion. "I wanted to wake up and see you. It was quite a jolt to reach for you and find that you were gone."

"Poor baby." He was so close, Venus felt his breath on her face. Did women swoon in the 1980s? "That must have been traumatic for you."

"There's that squeak in your voice again."

"Genetic flaw," she whispered. When Eli lowered his head and claimed her mouth with his, she really did think she was going to faint.

Eli let his mouth course along her cheek to her ear. He nipped the lobe gently. "Last night was wonderful. You know, I'm glad you haven't had a great deal of experience with men—though I damn well never thought it would be that important to me."

Venus was out of breath and off-balance, but even in the heat of Eli's embrace she could remember the bad experience she'd had with her one and only lover. It seemed unreal now, as though it had happened to someone else. Eli had wiped that time away.

"What is it? You trembled."

"It's nothing." She reached up and touched his cheek. "I'm glad I waited for . . . for the right time. You've brought a sweetness into my life."

Eli stared at her for long moments, his mouth softening in a smile. "As you have to mine. What we have is very special." He kissed her again, his mouth lingering. "Did you know that when you blush, it starts way down here?" Eli put his hand between her breasts, letting his fingers slide down her middle, moving lower.

Breathless, Venus pushed back from him, surprised that he could stir her passions so readily. "I have work to do." *I have to find out if you're a crook!* she thought with twinge of irony.

He extended his hand, his index finger tapping her nose. "One day, Venus, I'm going to know your secrets."

"And will I know yours?"

"Ask me anything."

Venus opened her mouth and shut it again. "I really need to get to work."

"Venus! It's Christmas Eve! Besides, you have five minutes until the office opens officially."

"Oh?" Would he suspect that her motivations were deeper than the average conscientious employee? Venus crossed her arms and leaned back in her chair. "And who's the boss here?"

Eli sat on the edge of her desk. "We haven't discussed any plans for the holidays. Would you like to dine at home tonight? Have a Christmas buffet and then decorate our tree?"

Although Venus was hesitant, she couldn't resist the chance to spend Christmas with Eli. "I'd like that."

"Me, too. We'll send Monihan off to visit his sister." He picked up a pencil and pointed it at her. "It's Christmas Eve. I want to spend it with you alone."

"Sounds good."

He nodded and his smile warmed her heart.

"But shouldn't you be with your family on Christmas Eve?" she asked. As Venus had lost her parents when she was a young girl, she usually spent the holidays with friends.

Eli shrugged. "Uncle Dismas is my only family, and he's planning to spend the weekend at a friend's lodge." He put his finger on her lips. "Don't fight me on this, Venus. I want you with me."

The net was closing! Why couldn't she fight him? Assert herself, assure her independence, put him off until she knew she could trust him . . . "All right."

They were interrupted by a knock at the door.

Eli didn't take his eyes from her as a messenger entered and handed her a package.

"Thank you." Venus placed the manila envelope on the wooden surface of the desk and turned toward her computer. "Have to get to work."

"You're a tough master. Going to study the Wade file?"

"Will that be a problem for you?" she countered warily.

He shook his head, his lopsided smile washing over her like an effervescent wave. "I'll see you later. And remember, boss, tomorrow is a holiday. We can spend the morning in bed . . . together."

She watched him stroll through the door leading to his office. Then she expelled a shaky sigh. Eli Weldon-Tate was a wondrous miracle in her life. If only she could keep him.

Eli's private line rang, interrupting the silence of his plush office. He settled himself in his sleek leather swivel chair. "Yes? Oh, Merry Christmas to you, Uncle Dismas. Thank you for the gift. I'll see you when you return, of course. Venus and I are spending the holidays together. Yes, it will be special for me. Give my best to Josh and Marian."

As Eli cradled the receiver, he sat back in his chair and gazed at the silver-wrapped package from Rothstein's. Would Venus like the scrolled gold

heart he'd bought her? Isaac Rothstein had se-
lected several pieces for Eli to choose from.

"Eli, my friend, it will cost the earth for that
piece. Those gems embedded in the gold are actually emerald-cut diamonds. Each diamond is worth
a great deal on its own. Isn't the work exquisite?"

"I'll take it . . . and I want to order a ring with
the diamond you described to me once—the one so
perfectly white that it has a violet hue."

"You're joking, chum. It's one of a kind, and we
never thought to sell it." Isaac grinned. "You'll
put your godson through Princeton with this. My
father will be downright giddy."

The blood thudded through Eli's veins, heavy
and out of rhythm. Venus! When he pictured himself giving her the gold heart he'd chosen for her
Christmas present, an inordinate happiness filled
him. He would have to be careful with her, not
rush her, but as soon as possible he wanted to give
her the engagement ring.

His enthusiasm shook him somewhat. He'd been
envisioning marriage to Venus since the day he'd
first met her. He'd never thought he would find a
woman who filled the great voids in his life. Despite all the business glitches nagging him, his
spirit, mind, and body were warm because Venus
was in his life.

Was it seconds or years that passed before Venus
picked up the manila envelope on her desk? Turning it in her hands, she wondered what it could be.

Her skin prickled when she opened it and saw
the sheaf of printouts with the Teague and Wayne
letterhead.

Facts and figures blurred before her eyes, her

skin turning clammy and shivery as a picture began to form.

The letter accompanying the printouts stated
that she was equally culpable in her partner's chicanery. The letter asked if she thought Eli Weldon-
Tate would want a person of uncertain business
reputation working so closely with him.

It was all too baffling! Last night Benedict had
hinted that Eli was entangled in wrongdoings.
But this note implied that *she* would be the one to
smear his good reputation if he discovered the
so-called truth.

The note continued, specifying that Venus could
escape prosecution if she mailed Jeremy's ledger to
the enclosed post box number as soon as possible.

It was all too strange. How did they know she
had Jeremy's ledger?

Venus had been slightly miffed to receive Jeremy's ledger in the mail back in October. She never
had a chance to ask him about it, as he was killed
the next day. Most of the scrawlings in the ledger
were illegible and cryptic, but she had been able
to decipher a few things. "Olympus" had appeared
more than once. And there were a few brokerage
houses in Orlando listed among the scribbled notes
and figures.

Oh, how she wished Jeremy had talked to her
about the ledger. No matter how hard she tried, it
had been impossible to make sense of his notes.
That had always been a minor bone of contention
between them. "Jeremy," she'd told him repeat-
edly, "write slower, clearer."

For long moments she sat there staring blindly
at the damaging papers. Her partner was dead.
This blackmailer could no longer hurt poor Jeremy, but how dare he try to blacken the memory

of her partner and friend! She'd paid her debts, and she had the loan payments and empty savings account to prove it. After studying the threatening documents, she put them back in the manila envelope. Later, at home, she would go over them again, and maybe find an answer or at least a clue to this new evil.

More determined than ever, Venus returned to her computer and tried to glean a clue from the files she'd pulled. She had worked through the one disk and had put in another when a name caught her eye. Meridian Investments of Orlando, Florida. Orlando! Wasn't that city mentioned in Jeremy's notebook?

Venus's curiosity was aroused. She'd have to take another look at the ledger, which was still in her safety deposit box.

She looked back at the computer screen. *Olympus . . . Orlando . . .*

A few times she'd been on the verge of calling Bahira, a friend in Orlando, to ask her about the strange references in Jeremy's ledger. Now there was a mention of Orlando in one of the Weldon-Tate files. Foolish coincidence?

Bahira! The name flashed into her mind. Bahira Massoud had been a classmate of Jeremy's and hers at Maxwell. Now the Moroccan woman was working at Epcot Center in Disney World. Venus wondered if Jeremy was in touch with Bahira before the accident. What kind of web had Jeremy been caught in? He had alluded to being over his head more than once, but Venus had always assumed that he was exaggerating.

Without pausing to think further, she reached for her purse and took out her address book. Dialing quickly, she crossed her fingers hoping that her friend might still be at home. No answer!

Taking a chance, she dialed information and asked for the phone number of Epcot Center. One more call, and she was put through to the Moroccan segment of the World Showcase.

"Hello? Bahira, is that you? Yes, it's Venus." Venus bit her lip, feeling teary. "It's so good to hear your voice . . ."

Venus sat with the dead phone in her hand, not hearing the signal that warned of a phone off the hook. Tears clogged her throat. She would have to leave Eli! It was time to face the inevitable. And the prospect of involving Bahira in a possible blackmailer's scheme didn't set well, either. Was she plummeting down a deep, dark well?

"Oh, Jeremy," she whispered in a hoarse voice. "What did you get yourself into?" Had he faced frightening horrors in his last days of life? Venus shivered at the thought. Everyone believed Jeremy's death was an accident, but now she was beginning to wonder . . .

Venus wasn't surprised that her partner had confided a few things in Bahira, but it seemed that he'd pulled her into the tangled web of danger.

Bahira had a ledger, too!

The Moroccan woman had described the cryptic book over the phone, and it sounded so much like the ledger in Venus's safety deposit box. Venus didn't understand the significance of either notebook, but she had one strong, instinctive feeling: She had to get to the bottom of this!

Although Bahira had offered to mail the ledger, Venus thought it wiser to fly down and pick it up. "We need to be careful," she'd told her friend.

"I'm afraid Jeremy was in over his head, and now someone is trying to clean up the evidence." She told Bahira about the shooting incident and the close call with the cab. Concern was evident in Bahira's voice when she warned her friend to take care. Before hanging up, they made plans to meet at the Orlando airport.

Get a grip on yourself! Venus thought as she finally replaced the telephone receiver and swiped at the tears lingering in her eyes. With a heartfelt sigh, she turned toward the screen and tried to concentrate on the figures swimming before her.

A moment later Eli opened the door, pausing to watch as she sat in front of her computer.

"Daydreaming?" He crossed to her quickly. "Hey, is that a tear on your cheek? Am I working you too hard?"

"No ... no, not at all." Venus turned in her swivel chair and reached up for him, her hands cupping his cheek. "I just needed to kiss you." Closing her burning eyes, she brushed her lips across his, wanting and needing the contact. She felt his body react in surprise, then he was meeting her vulnerable request with a sweeping passion.

Lifting her out of the chair, he pressed her to him, deepening the kiss. "Maybe we should make this a part of office procedure," he whispered with a sigh. "Let's go home. It's Christmas Eve, after all."

Venus was out of breath, her heart racing. "I have things to finish ... but we could leave early." The morning's search hadn't resolved anything, but she was hopeful. She hadn't found any accounts linking Eli to Olympus—or any other shady dealings. And she prayed that she never would.

"You're still daydreaming. About what?" Jealousy fired through him, shocking him. "Dammit!

I'm even jealous about your thoughts now. What are you doing to me, lady?"

Venus put her head on his shoulder for a moment, wanting nothing more than to stay in his arms. "You're jealous of Weldon-Tate? Isn't that a little counterproductive?"

"When you kiss me like that I could throw over the whole damned business."

Venus wiggled in his arms. "Ummm, think of tonight."

"I won't be able to think of anything else. The office closes at noon today. Get your work done." Eli kissed her hard, then replaced her in her chair. "We'll go home and put the finishing touches on the tree."

"Shouldn't we put in an extra hour or so?" She wanted to finish going through all the Olympus files.

"No!" Eli turned around and glared at her when she laughed. "It's Christmas Eve!" he called on his way out the door.

Venus's heart squeezed inside her as she thought of the holiday. Afterward, she would be leaving him. She had so much to do, so many odd details to research. And the first thing on her list was that ledger!

Glancing at her watch, she decided she had enough time to get down to the bank and back before anyone even knew she was gone.

Passing the receptionist, she smiled. "I'll be back in a few minutes, Deena, if anyone wants me. Take my calls, will you?"

"Sure will, Venus."

Since it was Christmas Eve there were very few customers in the bank. She was able to get into her safety deposit box quickly and retrieve the notebook she sought. She had to take Jeremy's ledger to Florida with her. With Bahira's help, she might be able to make some sense of what Jeremy had been trying to say in the ledgers. In minutes, she was on her way back to Weldon-Tate, running.

Still a little breathless, she stepped from the elevator and passed the receptionist. "Messages?"

"None, Venus." Deena smiled.

Good, Venus thought. Now all she had to do was make her flight reservations.

Venus could barely keep her mind on her work as she fretted about the necessity of getting on an airplane on the day after Christmas. She had two days with Eli . . . today and tomorrow. They would be the most beautiful, most poignant days of her life. Finding Eli, and now losing him so soon . . . Venus didn't like facing that, but she could't confide in Eli yet. And she would have to accept that losing him was a possibility. This was something she would have to take care of alone.

The rest of the morning flew by as Venus immersed herself in her new project: tracking down executives of the Olympus Corporation. It was puzzling and frustrating. How could a corporation hide its personnel and still trade so actively on the stock market?

Marking the disk she'd been compiling on Olympus with an X, she put it into her side drawer instead of the disk file she normally used. She didn't want this information falling into the wrong hands. By the time she cleared off her desk, Venus's head ached with all the unanswered questions.

Pain lanced her at the thought of separating from Eli. It was as though all the happiness in the world mushroomed into her life when he'd entered

it. Now that explosion of happiness would give
way to lonely darkness.

Closing her drawer, she locked it and put the
key in her purse.

Eli stood in the doorway of her office, watching
her graceful movements. She was so beautiful! He
had known beautiful women before, some very
sultry and sexy, but none of them had captivated
him as Venus had done. "Ready?" he asked, pushing away from the doorjamb.

Startled, she pulled her hands away from the
drawer she'd just locked and turned to look at
him. Her smile made his chest tighten and all else
disappear from his mind.

"Let's go. We have a tree to decorate."

A fragrant Norwegian spruce had appeared in
Eli's living room the previous day. "Where did
Monihan get such a big one? Do you have enough
ornaments for it?"

Eli shrugged. "He purchased extra ornaments
before he left to visit with his sister. You know he
won't be back until the day after Christmas. Should
we take that day off and stay in bed?"

Venus's heart knotted. She would be on her way
to Florida. Her heart was heavy with fear and
treachery. Trying to hide her face to mask her
sudden guilt, she bent down to retrieve her purse.
"Not a good idea with so much work to be done
here. I'm ready."

Eli sensed her tension as they took the executive
elevator to the garage below the Weldon-Tate Building. "Is something wrong?"

Venus looked up at him. "I . . . I just want us to
have the best Christmas Eve ever."

Eli sucked in a breath at the pain in her eyes. "I

guarantee it." Hooking an arm around her, he brought her to his side, his chin resting on her hair. "Do you know how happy you've made me since we met?"

"As happy as you've made me?"

"We make a good team."

They walked out of the elevator, arms around each other.

Neither saw the car heading toward them until the last moment.

"Jee-zus!" With lightning speed, Eli lifted Venus and fell back against another car. "Damn these holiday drinkers! Are you all right?" He slid off the hood of the Mercedes, still clutching her.

"Yes . . . yes. Are you?"

Noting the anxiety behind her smile, Eli shot a sharp glance in the direction the car had gone, then back at Venus. Had it been an accident? He cursed himself for failing to get the license plate number. With the tinted windows, he'd been unable to see the driver of the black Cadillac.

All at once, both of them were lost in their own troubled thoughts. They got into the car, drove out of the garage, and made their way through the Manhattan traffic to Eli's place.

So the plot thickens, Venus thought. The close call in the parking garage was the third such incident in the last month. Although neither she nor Eli wanted to admit the truth, they both knew it had been no accident.

The only consolation for Venus was the fact that Eli had been by her side. The driver could have just as easily harmed him. It was a new piece of evidence in his favor, attesting to his innocence.

Tears burned her throat as she stole a glimpse of the man beside her. Like a condemned woman buying time, she vowed to cherish these last, glorious days with him. It was time to store all the moments, hoard the precious wonder of his love, so that she could treasure the memory for the rest of her life.

They stepped into the private elevator and the doors closed, speeding them to the apartment. Venus didn't realize how tense she'd been until she exhaled in relief.

"It's good to be home," Eli whispered in her ear.

"Yes." She turned in his arms and looked up at him, her head cocked to one side. "Let's take this holiday slowly. I want to savor every moment."

Alarm bells went off in Eli's head. Why did he have the sudden dread of a wrenching loss? Ridiculous! He had to forget his foolish thoughts. Tonight was Christmas Eve . . . with Venus. "We can have a late dinner. We don't need to open our gifts until midnight."

"Oh! But I didn't get you anything."

"Ah, but you did. Having you here with me is all the Christmas I need."

"I . . . I used to go to St. Patrick's on Christmas Eve." More often than not she'd gone to the cavernous church alone. The only solace had been the solemn service and powerful music. Though Venus always had good friends as well as work that absorbed her, she'd often suffered from bouts of loneliness. Many times, in the church, she'd found a measure of peace.

"We can do that. I'd like that. I used to go to St. Bart's with my uncle." Eli kissed her nose. "But first, let's hit the showers."

"My, you're anxious." Venus laughed when he swept her into his arms and took the stairs two at a time. "And strong."

"Able to leap tall buildings, et cetera, since I met you."

Venus pushed her face into his neck, blotting out everything but Eli from her mind.

The shower took eons . . . or minutes. The love-making was timeless.

In the shower they had laved each other's bodies with the fragrant soap. Now, in bed, they massaged and caressed each other with passionate hands. Love was a kaleidoscope that carried them away, wrapping them in a color wheel of sensuous need.

Venus forgot her icy dread over leaving Eli, for she was overwhelmed by the fiery need to have him and keep him.

Then all reason faded and there was only Eli.

Venus turned to liquid as she pressed against him. Had it been a hundred years since they'd made love? Would she ever have enough of the wonder of Eli Weldon-Tate?

"What are you thinking, beautiful one?" Eli's voice was slurred.

"Of how much I want you." Venus's hands feathered over his strong, masculine chest, plucking gently at the hair there. How familiar he seemed! As though she'd been joined to Eli for ages. His arousal not only inflamed her, it gave her joy.

"You excite me so much." Eli's voice was muffled against her. "You have such a wonderful body. No one ever had lovelier breasts." His mouth followed the whispered words, touching the nipples with his tongue.

Did Eli have a magic? Venus felt more beautiful when she was with him. The pores of her skin seemed to take fire when he touched her. Did her eyes take on a purple sparkle? Did her hair shine with more luster because he was beside her? Was Eli a special vitamin? Venus chuckled.

"Tell me the joke." He kissed her.

Venus threaded her fingers through his hair. "You make me feel . . . well, healthy. That sounds silly, huh?"

"No, it's true, because you do the same for me. I need you. You're my special elixir of life, lady." He leaned back from her. "I never thought there was anyone like you on the planet, and I'm so damned grateful to have found you." His lips caressed her abdomen and thighs, making her stomach muscles clench in delight. He moved down her body until his tongue was caressing her instep.

The loveplay inflamed Eli. Never had he needed someone so much. Never had a woman given him so much joy . . . not just joy but old-fashioned happiness. With Venus he could pursue amusement with the same dedication he'd always applied to business. While he was loving her with an earth-shaking passion, he wanted to laugh and shout with the joy of living. Venus!

To Venus, making love with Eli was like all the wonderful thrills of birthday and Christmas rolled up in one. It was so joyous. Happiness coursed through her like a raging river.

An ecstasy filled her as Eli resumed his journey up her body once more. Nothing had ever come close to the fire he'd built inside her. Her skin became a thousand sensors that flashed heat and passion to the very core of her. "Don't . . . don't leave me, Eli." The words burst unbidden from her throat.

"I never will, darling. Never." His mouth went down her body again, slower, more intense in his love search.

"Stop, Eli, I'm ready."

"Not yet, love. I want to make up for those long years before I met you."

"Silly man." Her words were as slurred as his.

With one strong arm he positioned her under him, murmuring sweet promises against her skin, over and over.

His gentle plunge transfixed them both until a rhythm took them and spiraled them away.

"Venus! Darling!"

Locked together in desperate love, they took each other out beyond the stars.

"I love you, Venus."

"I love you, Eli."

Mouth-to-mouth, the covenants were whispered, their arms tightening as though they must be forever one.

Chapter Six

Venus pressed her face against the window of the airplane that roared through the sky toward Orlando.

It was a beautiful day to fly. The sun was shining, the sky was a cap of blue and white coldness that made the eye teary.

Spending Christmas with Eli seemed like a distant memory. She fingered the gold heart at her throat, loving the smooth surface.

What was he doing now? Asleep still? He had been lightly snoring when she left, so deep in sleep that she'd been sure she could have slammed doors and not disturbed him. But Venus had taken every precaution after their long night of love and had slipped out quietly.

Despite her fatigue, she hadn't been able to sleep, knowing that when day broke she would be gone. Venus had lain awake, wanting only to touch him, to be close to him. At dawn she'd risen from the bed.

Creeping down the stairs, even though she knew that Monihan would not return until later in the day, she'd called for a taxi from the phone in the study. Then she'd lifted her two light bags and taken the elevator to the garage, the yellow light of the enclosed area making her tremble.

It hadn't been too much of an effort to get by the
security guard on duty. She'd waited until he'd
left his kiosk to go on rounds and walked up the
ramp to the sidewalk. Manhattan was still in darkness when she'd huddled into her coat, waiting for
the cab. Her shivers were as much from fear of
discovery as from cold . . . and the terrible reaction of leaving Eli.

Venus barely remembered the ride through the
tunnel and along the expressway to La Guardia
Airport. She had boarded the aircraft with a mini-
mum of fuss, but the farther away from Eli she
went, the more his face loomed clear before her.

Christmas! Had there ever been such a festive
holiday? She fingered the filigreed gold heart at
her throat. Venus had been tempted to return the
charm to Eli, knowing that she would be leaving
him, but she hadn't been able to do it.

Each time they'd made love, he'd kissed the
golden charm. "That's my heart you have, darling.
It's yours forever."

The passion between them had been all-consuming,
lasting, growing. Even thinking of him now, her
body grew warm and pliant. There wasn't one
inch of her body that he hadn't loved. And when
her back had arched in ultimate ecstasy, he'd been
there with her, his whispered words of love meeting hers, mouth to mouth, soul to soul.

"Breakfast, miss?"

Venus looked around at the flight attendant in
surprise, too bemused to refuse the food that she
didn't want. "Thank you."

"Traveling on business?" asked the man next to
her. He tilted his head, his voice friendly.

Venus was about to nod her head when she noticed the attention of the man across the aisle.

Had she ever seen that bespectacled man before? A vision of the same man on a Manhattan street jumped into her mind. Was that the man who'd pushed her into the path of the cab? No! It was her imagination playing tricks. This was a businessman with a briefcase open on the seat next to him. There were more than a few men wearing glasses in Manhattan.

"Yes, I'm on business." Venus bent over her food, pushing it around the plastic plate with the cold utensils. She drank the coffee and juice, took a forkful of egg, then picked up her own briefcase from the floor and opened it.

Jeremy's ledger was there. Leafing through it, she once more went over the hen scratchings that her partner had called his shorthand, but she could make nothing of it. She stared at scrawled words and unfinished sentences until the scribbles blurred and she dropped off to sleep.

Eli was a madman.

Wide-eyed, Monihan watched him, his suitcases at his feet. The boss had been like that since the moment he'd walked into the kitchen. Monihan flinched when the kitchen phone was almost ripped from the wall. "Boss, if you'd just let me—"

"I can't find her."

Monihan's words faded away as he saw the pain in his employer's eyes. "I'll talk to my people, boss."

Eli tried to smile, but couldn't. Shaking his head, he put his head on the other man's shoulder. "Thank you. I don't mean to take this out on you. But, this woman . . . she means the world to me—"

"Is that so?"

"Close your mouth, man. I love the woman."

"I knew it had to be some sort of craziness." Monihan shook his head, his face thoughtful. "Have you thought of calling your uncle? It amazes me what he knows about things, sir, if you know what I mean."

"Dismas? Why not? I'll go to the office and see what I can find out there. You call my uncle and tell him to get back to me immediately—if not sooner. I'm leaving now."

"In your pajama bottoms? Unshaven? You'd create quite a stir, I'm thinkin."

"Damn you, Monihan, get my uncle." Eli left the room at a run.

Moving along with the throng of workers streaming into the Weldon-Tate Building was like being part of a stampede. People were cattle that had to be manipulated and controlled.

From what he'd seen of Venus Wayne, she was always early, but there was no sign of her at the moment. Maybe there was time to take a look in her office. With luck, the ledger would be there. It wasn't in her old apartment . . . and after all the trouble he'd gone through to pull that place apart!

Jeremy Teague had been a fool, but a fool for detail. He'd kept extensive records of everything. Stupid fool! No doubt Venus Wayne had all his records. But where?

He fingered the metal tool in his pocket. The motion helped to calm his burgeoning anger. His original plan to steal a key had been scrapped. Too chancy. Caution was the byword. Enemies would be destroyed. The world bowed to determination.

Getting off the elevator with a few other people, he mixed with the crowd and went unnoticed. Others were engrossed with self. Most were yawning, some were reading the morning paper. Lack of observation destroyed people!

If pretty little Venus Wayne were found dead in her chair, Eli Weldon-Tate would look bad. Maybe he would even be charged with murder! What a pleasant idea.

Using the tool that had the configuration of a nail file, he tripped the lock and entered the woman's office.

The early morning sunlight slanted across her desk, glittering along the gold caps of her pens and on her notepad. Crossing to the desk, he lightly scratched a pencil across the indentations on the notepad. His work revealed the information: the airline and a strange name.

An early morning flight to Orlando! What the hell . . .

Pretty little Venus Wayne! What was she after in Florida? Had she taken Teague's records with her? Or was she picking them up? Teague had spent a lot of time in Orlando. Too much time! The blasted man had kept too many secrets, too many records!

In one angry motion he tore the message from the pad and crept toward the door.

Take a deep breath. Don't hurry. Don't slam doors on the way to the elevator. Pretty Venus Wayne was trying to be smart, ignoring his letter! Well, she would soon find that she couldn't pull tricks like that and get away with it.

Eli touched the corner of his chin where he'd nicked himself shaving. Damn! Where was she? His anger warred with concern as he rode in the private elevator up to his office.

It was damned lonely without her. He'd grown accustomed to being with Venus in the morning . . . and at work . . . and in the evening.

His fist hitting the wall of the elevator made a resounding boom.

When the door opened into his office, he crossed the room rapidly and headed down the hall toward Venus's office. Her desk was cleared, the way she'd left it on Christmas Eve. He strode to her empty chair and rubbed the leather back. "Where did you go, damn you?"

All at once a nameless dread assailed him. He'd had the feeling that Venus was hiding something from him. Damn her for not talking to him about her fears. If only . . .

The phone peeled at his elbow, startling him. He picked it up on the first ring. "Yes? Dismas? Listen, Venus is gone. I think she's in trouble."

"Don't panic, my boy, she's on a flight to Orlando. From what I've been able to glean, she has a friend down there and—"

"So, you've been up to your old tricks." Irritation and relief warred within him, making him raise his voice.

"Let's put it this way: Since you've had a few threats on your life since Black Monday, I've had a guard on you."

"I see."

"That cold tone doesn't daunt me, my boy. You should know that by now. One of my men began following Venus because it looked as though she had become the target of some unfriendly happenings that could ricochet onto you."

"Then she *is* in trouble."

"I would say that she is as safe in Orlando as she was here. Safer, maybe."

"I'm going to Florida."

"Now, Eli—"

"Uncle, you get yourself into my office and stay

here. You are now officially in charge of Weldon-Tate Enterprises."

"I'm retired," Dismas informed him mildly.

"And you've been chomping at the bit to get back in the saddle."

"True." After a moment's hesitation, Dismas said, "I'll be in later today, my boy. What are your plans?"

"I'll be on the next plane to Florida. Get in touch with your man and have him meet me up at the airport. What's his name?"

"It's Spider, but, Eli—"

"Get on it. Good-bye, Uncle."

Orlando was teeming with Christmas visitors passing through the airport in pell-mell streams.

Having carried both her bags off the plane, Venus now stood looking around her.

"Venus! Here." Bahira was waving as she crossed the maelstrom of people in the airport corridor.

Venus dropped her bags to enclose her diminutive friend in a bear hug. "I've missed you."

"I've missed you, too, Venus." Bahira stared at her. "You have a new, healthy look about you. I've never seen you so glowing, your eyes so—"

"You're just happy to see me, chum." Venus bent to snatch up her bag, trying to control the flush that she knew was spreading across her face. Bahira had always been too perceptive.

Bahira took one of Venus's bags and hooked arms with her. "Honestly, Venus, I've never seen you look better. Got a sexy hunk in your life?"

Venus pretended to be indignant. "I don't know what your parents would say if they could hear your 'slanguage.' All those tutors shot to hell."

Bahira laughed out loud. "You're the cause of it all. You and Jeremy."

Both women were silent for a moment as they remembered their ebullient friend.

"Even if he did believe in cutting too close to the law, I liked him," Bahira murmured. "In many ways he was the smartest one in our class."

"He certainly kept the most notes." Venus shot a quick glance at her friend, who nodded slowly. "Do you think that our ledgers will tell us what was on Jeremy's mind?"

"I have a feeling they will. If I know Jeremy— and we both did—then he listed everything. Jeremy was a detail-oriented man."

The two women maneuvered around a motorized cart, then came together again.

"You're right, Bahira. He was a great one to chronicle things and keep close track of every occurrence."

Bahira shook her head. "But he had a fatal addiction to taking big chances. Remember the mock business we set up for our thesis at Maxwell?" Bahira gestured toward an exit.

"How could I forget? He would have gone bust if we hadn't caught him up. But he had very good instincts about choosing a business. Remember that? Our study group got the highest grade."

Bahira grimaced. "That's because you and I burned the midnight oil to put it all together." She sighed. "Jeremy was a wild man at times. That's why I'm afraid he might have gotten in too deep and put himself at risk. You know they play for keeps on Wall Street."

Venus followed her friend through a sliding door. "But Jeremy was very smart about the financial game." She shook her head. "I don't know. It doesn't seem possible that so much has happened, that Jeremy's dead. If only he hadn't gotten himself involved with . . . such dangerous people."

"I think you're starting to come around to my thinking, Venus." Bahira looked grim. "I've thought from the start that Jeremy's death might not have been an accident."

"Bahira!"

"Whether you accept it on the surface or not, Venus, a part of you has been questioning his death from the start. I know you."

Venus bit her lip. It was true.

"Even if he did believe in cutting too close to the law, he was our friend," Bahira murmured. "And no one had a right to hurt him."

"You're right."

The two women stowed the luggage in the back of Bahira's truck. "How do you like my vehicle, Venus?"

"A truck?" Venus looked at the Isuzu and smiled. "I can't imagine the prince thinking this an adequate vehicle for his daughter."

"He wouldn't. But it suits me." Bahira climbed in and started the truck. Putting it in gear, she moved slowly out of the parking area to the access road. "I sensed the urgency in your voice on the phone. So instead of going to the apartment first, I thought that we should go straight to Epcot, where I've hidden Jeremy's ledger."

"That uncanny clairvoyance of yours told you it was important. Correct?"

Bahira nodded slowly. "It doesn't take a psychic to figure out how important this matter is."

Venus had never seen her friend look so concerned. "Let's get your ledger and put the two of them together, then."

"By the way, in the notebook Jeremy sent me, there's a notation about Blue Spring Park. That's in Orange City, not too far from here. But I didn't understand the reference. So much of his writing is impossible to read."

"Isn't it? I couldn't make out much of his in my ledger."

"Who could ever really understand Jeremy and everything he did. There were so many levels to him."

"True." Venus's mind wandered back to the last times she'd been with her partner . . .

"Venus, honey, don't worry," he'd assured her. "We'll be all right. I've got enough stuff hidden away to cover any losses."

"You mean money?"

"Better. I have information stashed from here to Florida."

What had Jeremy meant?

Round and round she went, but there were no clear answers.

"Venus? Come out of the daydream you've been in; I thought you'd fallen sleep. We're almost there."

Venus shook herself out of the reverie and looked around her. "Where are we?"

Bahira laughed. "Almost to our destination. See, there's the entrance to Disney World. Big, isn't it?"

"Very."

"I feel very tense about this, Venus, as though we're turning the key on Pandora's box."

"Now you know how I've felt since that packet arrived in my office."

"Hmmm," Bahira mused, staring into the rearview mirror. "I guess I was wrong. I thought that guy was going to drive right into the parking lot with us. He's been tailing us for a while."

Venus looked over her shoulder and saw a Cadillac with tinted glass speeding away. "I thought tinted glass was illegal?"

"It is. Come on, we'll walk from here, then take the boat across. The Moroccan Showcase is right at the boat livery."

Eli had a feeling he could have flown faster than the plane. He alternately wanted to strangle Venus and make love to her until she was incapable of running away from him. Deep concern over her safety made him edgy and irritable. He cursed the hapless pilot who announced to the passengers that they had a tail wind and that he expected to arrive in Orlando only fifteen minutes behind schedule.

Once in the airport, Eli headed for the lower level. He was running his finger down the illuminated directory of car rental companies when someone touched his elbow.

"Mr. Weldon-Tate? I'm Spider."

Eli straightened slowly, his hand leaving the directory and clenching into a fist. "Haven't I seen you around the firm?"

The bespectacled man in the rumpled black suit nodded. "Yep."

"And you work for my uncle?"

"Yep. I got a Caddy outside. You wanna go right to where Miss Wayne is?"

"Yes, as quickly as possible. Is she all right?"

"She was when I saw her with her friend. They spotted me, so I had to cut away from them for a few miles, but then I picked them up again." The man frowned. "They went in a boat. I walked around the lake—don't like boats—saw them go into the Moroccan Showcase." He shrugged. "But if they aren't there when we go back, I know where her friend lives."

"Good. Take me to where you last saw her. Let's go."

Spider led the way to a black car with tinted windows parked in a yellow crossing zone. "Told 'em it was an emergency," he explained blandly when Eli looked at him.

"I see." Where did Dismas find the people who worked for him?

They sped out of the airport parking lot as though jet propelled. But Eli was not disconcerted at the speed with which Spider drove; he welcomed it.

"Dismas says you're worried about Miss Wayne."

"I am."

"No need. I've been watching her."

"So I understand," Eli responded dryly.

"And I'm good at what I do," Spider said simply. They wheeled around a slower-moving vehicle in one lane, then passed a convertible on the inside lane.

When they arrived at their destination Eli stared at the stream of people pouring toward the entrance to Epcot. "This is a damned busy place. Easy to lose your mark here."

"Yes, it is. But Dismas trusts me."

Eli looked askance at the immutable Spider. "The inference is that I should?"

"Up to you." Spider parked the big car with a screech of brakes and a spray of gravel. "This way." Spider was out of the car, moving fast around people to get to the turnstiles.

Eli might have been in a city dump for all the impression these beautiful surroundings made on him.

Both men broke into a fast jog through throngs of people, past the varied points of interest.

"We can go around or—"

"I'll take the boat. It's just leaving now. If you spot her, give me a signal." Eli ran and leaped on board just before the small ferry cast off. His eyes roved everywhere, hoping to spot Venus. He was going to find her—come hell or high water.

Venus shook her head. "I have no idea what yours means either, Bahira."

Her friend sighed. "Jeremy's writing is atrocious."

The two sat at a small table in the back room of the Moroccan World Showcase. Venus stabbed at a notation in Bahira's ledger. "There's another mention of Blue Spring Park. Could those markings next to it be a drawing? Like a house?"

Bahira leaned forward. "Could be . . ." She pressed two fingers against her forehead as though she tried to call up an image. "Wait a minute. When Jeremy was down here, he mentioned that he had a second cousin who was a park ranger, although I don't know if they were close."

Venus sat forward, leaning over Jeremy's tiny drawing. "Unless it's just a pencil mark, it looks like there's an arrow pointing to the chimney." Venus sat back with a sigh. "It's a long shot, but we don't have anything else to go on, Bahira. I'm going to that park . . . now. What was the cousin's name?"

"I don't know." Bahira shook her head and frowned. "I can't go with you. I have to work."

"Draw me a map and lend me your truck. I can't wait on this. May I take your ledger?"

"It's yours." The Moroccan woman stood, following Venus from the back room. "Be careful. I have bad feelings about this."

"It's just that wild desert blood of yours." Venus took her friend's keys, kissed her cheek, and hurried from the pavilion.

Out of breath from running, Eli hooked up with

Spider on the edge of the parking lot. Neither man took his eyes from Venus as she hurried toward the gates of Epcot. Eli sensed rather than saw the man at his side. "I don't want to lose her."

"We won't," Spider said.

They ran to the Cadillac just as Venus was wheeling out of the parking lot.

Eli kept his eyes glued to the truck Venus was driving. Fortunately, she seemed unsure of her direction and didn't drive that fast once she was on the highway. That helped Spider keep her in sight.

Where the hell was she going?

Was she running, frightened and intimidated? The very thought turned Eli's blood to ice. He knew that something or someone had catapulted her into this trip. He didn't like the idea of anything threatening her.

Fear coated his mouth as he tried to envision what it could be. Damn her! She needed to be with him so that he could protect her from harm. He hated this feeling of helplessness, this battle with an unknown evil. Why hadn't she come to him with her fears? Hadn't he shown her in their lovemaking that he was committed to her, that he wanted to care for her?

He had to trust his instincts. They hadn't let him down when he'd fought in the war-torn jungles of Vietnam. And right now his instincts were shrieking with one thought: He was in love. In love with a recalcitrant redhead with incongruously hued violet eyes. Venus! He would keep her safe.

One village ran into another until they came to a town called Orange City.

When Venus turned down a road that led into Blue Spring Park, Eli straightened. His spine tin-

gled with a wariness he couldn't quite pinpoint.
Why was she here?

Venus could feel her upper lip beading with perspiration. What would she find here? Clues about
Jeremy? Had she ever really known him?

Every few moments her thoughts drifted back to
Eli. What was he doing now? Cursing her? He
couldn't have forgotten her already—could he? Even
if he didn't forget her right away, had he already
pushed her out of his life?

Her hand went up to the gold heart he'd given
her for Christmas. "I love you, Eli." Saying it out
loud was such a relief. She had loved him that
first moment when he'd tackled her in the lobby,
protecting her with his body.

So many times she'd wanted to remind him that
she was independent, that she made her own decisions. Had Eli even once interfered with that? Not
really. He'd tried only to stand between her and
harm's way. No one had ever given her that sense
of freedom that comes from real loving. She'd had
to get away from Eli to really see him, to know
him.

Now she was here in Blue Spring Park to find
out about her past with Jeremy and the business.
Had she tossed away the future by doing that?
Ineffable sadness filled her at the prospect of never
being with Eli again.

Shaking off her gloomy thoughts, she pulled up
to the ranger station to pay her fee to enter the
park. She smiled at the ranger. "Hello. A friend of
mine by the name of Jeremy Teague had a cousin
who works here . . ."

"We have a Teague." The ranger glanced at his
schedule. "She's patrolling the tributary this morning, I think. You can ask at Thursby House. They
would know."

"Thank you." Venus's skin goose-bumped in trepidation as she followed the winding road to the parking area not far from the manatee overlook and Thursby House. She wanted answers, but she was afraid of what she might uncover.

A few yards behind her in the Cadillac, Eli and Spider hadn't said much since entering the park. After they stopped the car behind a small hillock, they got out and stood under the shelter of a tree.

"There she is. I'll follow her."

"And I'll look around," Spider muttered, his head swiveling back and forth.

Trying to stay hidden, Eli ambled across the expanse of grass between the parking lot and the river. Why had she come here alone? Was she meeting someone? Jealousy flooded through him. Venus Wayne was able to conjure such deep feelings in him. Her power over him was remarkable.

Eli Weldon-Tate had been on his own since his late teens. He'd made business decisions involving worldwide conglomerates from the time he'd been in his mid-twenties. And now, with one glance from those violet eyes, Venus had come along and pulled the rug out from under him. She made him laugh. She inspired a fear he'd never known. She plumbed the depths of his being with a passion that had shaken him to the core. Venus was a witch! And he loved her.

Following a small cluster of people, Venus meandered toward a wooden overlook. It was sunny, a bit cool for Florida, and most people wore heavy jackets or coats.

She had to find out which ranger was Jeremy's relative. She would ask the first ranger she saw to direct her.

The first sign on the wooden bridge to the overlook described the manatee as a giant mammal, also known as a sea elephant. The ancient Greeks thought them mermaids. Another sign warned visitors to beware of the alligators. Venus shivered.

She was looking around her for a ranger when her attention was caught by the huge creatures moving so easily through the tributary. How graceful and slow moving they were!

She was about to turn away and go back to the place on the hill called Thursby House when she heard a commotion.

"Hey, that kid fell off the log! He's in the water with the manatee!"

Venus wasn't too concerned. According to the sign, the creatures posed no danger.

"I can't swim," a woman screamed. "Neither can my boy!"

Venus pushed through the throng of people clustered at the rail, watching.

"He'll drown! Help my boy!" The agonized voice cut the clear air like a scythe. The woman tried to jump into the water after the child but was restrained by the people on shore.

Where were the rangers? Venus kept her eyes on the boy as she removed her jacket.

A bearded man pointed to the small log floating just out of reach of the boy. "That's what he fell off." His glance slanted toward Venus as she began removing her shoes.

The large mammals with the elephantlike skin moved lazily, as though unaware there was a struggling alien in their midst. Now and then they came up to breathe, expelling water from their blowholes.

The bearded man blinked when Venus climbed the railing. "I'd go in for him, but I don't swim

that well. Besides, alligators come up this tributary. I've seen them on land and in the water.
Gotta be careful."

Alligators! Some distance away a person in dark
clothing lurked in the swampy underbrush. A long,
thick branch would be a goad and act as protection at the same time. Pretty little Venus Wayne
needed a swimming companion.

Facing the amphibious holdover from the dino-
saur age was a harrowing moment, but the gator
didn't seem too canny. Using the stick as a prod,
he urged the sluggish gator into the tributary.

"Hey, you! What are you doing with that gator?
Didn't you hear the alarm? There's a kid in that
water!"

Turning around with stick in hand and putting
everything behind the blow, the person leveled the
unsuspecting ranger, who never knew what hit him.

"That boy needs help now." Venus fixed on the
floundering youngster in the middle of the narrow
waterway. "Send someone for help, mister." Venus
slid out of her slacks.

"I'll get the rangers, lady. Be careful."

"Hurry. That boy might need first aid once I get
him out of there."

"I hope no alligators join you," the bearded man
muttered, pointing to the warning sign on the shore.

Venus shivered. She would try not to think of
that possibility. With one quick movement, she
was over the wooden rail and diving into the water, hitting clumsily and hard.

Expecting a shock of cold, she was surprised at
the relative warmth of the water. No wonder Flo-
ridians swam in December! The water was close to

July temperature for up north. At once she could feel the strong tug of the current.

Shooting to the surface, Venus stroked hard and straight for the child, who was more than halfway across the waterway, almost in the center of the throng of manatee. The boy was in the first stages of panic, thrashing and taking water.

Gathering her body into a ball, Venus snapped it straight out in a surface dive that took her down toward the child. What she saw almost made her lose the air she'd garnered in her system. A monster of a manatee, many thousands of pounds, was almost in front of her. A calf lingered at its side, between her and the child.

Lungs bursting, she thrust around the creature, bracing herself for a strike of some kind from the mother mammal. It didn't come. Her outstretched arms sought and found the sinking child.

It shocked her when she felt a lifting motion as she fought to get the child to the surface. A manatee had helped her? Impossible. Wasn't it?

Almost blacking out from lack of air, Venus broke the surface, barely hearing the many cheers as she gulped precious oxygen into her lungs.

Venus did hear the hurrahs turn to cries of horror and warning.

"Alligator! Alligator!"

Chapter Seven

Venus stared at the two eyes coming toward her. Even from a distance they had a cold malevolence. They were red! Did the sun make them that way?

The alligator was a distance away, but it had seen her. Without the unconscious child in her arms she might have been able to make it, but she couldn't swim quickly while toting the inert child. And she couldn't consider abandoning the burden in her arms.

Venus heard a splash as though someone had entered the water, but she didn't take her eyes off the alligator as she tried to increase her speed.

"Hurry, lady." Someone shouted. Others took up the cry. "Hurry!"

Venus strained to increase her speed. They still had a chance!

"That's all right, darling, don't be afraid. Keep going."

At the sound of Eli's voice, Venus swallowed water. "Eli! Don't! The alligator." She coughed and choked but didn't lessen her speed. Now fear crawled through her mind in a different way. Her darling Eli was confronting the alligator! Again he was between her and danger.

Suddenly he was gone, swimming toward the carnivore coming straight at him.

No! No! Not Eli! Gathering all her strength, Venus pulled hard to shore. Get the child to safety. Eli needed her. Eli! Eli! She had to help him. Hurry! Hurry!

At last she was at the soggy bank, passing the child to a helpful onlooker. As soon as the child was taken, Venus turned away, going back the way she'd come, back to Eli.

She was halfway there when she saw the thrashing in the water. "Eli! Oh, God!"

"I'm here, darling. The park rangers have netted him. It's all right. Let me take you to shore."

"Oh, Eli, I thought it had gotten you." Venus grasped him convulsively, sobbing.

For a moment they slipped underwater, locked in each other's arms. "Are you going to drown us?" he asked. But he was laughing. It made him so happy to see her, to hold her. "Don't cry, sweetheart."

"Even if we drown I won't let you go." Venus clutched him as they sank again.

When they broke the surface once more, Eli kissed her. "You risked your life for that boy. I couldn't get to you before you were into the water. You scared the hell out of me. I won't let you go. I told you that on Christmas and I meant it." He steered her back to shore, then lifted her and carried her up onto the riverbank.

When they were safely ashore, Eli gently lowered Venus to a bed of soft grass. Still breathless from the incident, they held each other in a desperate embrace. When they gazed into each other's eyes, it was as if they were alone, sequestered on a secluded island, surrounded only by swaying palm trees, a brilliant tropical sun, and wild marshlands.

A moment later, a ranger's voice reminded them that they were not alone on an island but surrounded by tourists in a state park.

"Sir, why don't you come this way. We've opened up the house and have a fire going in one of the big stoves. An emergency crew is there. They'll check both of you out after they're through with the boy."

"How is he?"

"Good, miss, thanks to you. Getting him out of there as fast as you did probably saved his life."

"I think I had help."

"You mean this gentleman?"

"Yes, but I also mean the giant manatee who pushed me to the surface. Don't look so disbelieving, Ranger. I was down pretty deep. I don't know if I had the air to get to the top—then I felt a nudge. It's true."

"Never mind that now, darling. We have to dry off." Eli took the towels from the ranger, glaring at the man who was eyeing Venus. Eli wrapped her up quickly.

"But the manatee did help me, Ranger."

"Well, ma'am, Ranger Teague was the first there. She said you were close to Doc and Emma and one of her calves." The park ranger hurried along next to them. "One of 'em helped you to the surface, huh? That's something."

"Where is Ranger Teague? Do you think I might speak to her?"

"I don't see why not. You get warmed up and I'll go get her."

"Thanks." Venus nodded, trying to stem the shivers that assailed her as she and Eli entered the house.

Once inside, she turned to Eli. Although her teeth were still chattering, she managed a smile. "I'm so glad to see you. Where did you come from? How did you find me?"

"When I get you warmed up, I'll be glad to show you just how I feel about seeing you again. But before I make love to you for twenty-four hours, I'm going to kill you for leaving me in the first place."

Venus touched his face with trembling fingers. "Eli, you don't understand . . ."

"I understand that we need to talk, to open up to each other, Venus! And we're going to do that. I was so damned worried!"

A woman ranger approached her, smiling. "That boy is going to be fine because of you, ma'am."

"Not a bad day's work, love," Eli whispered in her ear.

"Thank you for helping me." Venus gazed up at him, not trying to hide the deep emotion on her face. "My white knight rescued me from the monster." Tears stung her eyes, and her smile wobbled. "You could have been killed, Eli."

"So could you. Damn you, Venus." He kissed her hard.

The ranger coughed. "If you'll follow me, I'll show you where you can wash up."

Eli nodded, lifting his head. His gut reaction was to scoop Venus up and carry her to Tahiti, but he merely watched as the door closed behind her.

"Ah, sir, if you'd come this way you'll dry off better in here. I'm Ranger Dwayne."

Eli accompanied the other man into a small room, the heat from the iron stove very welcome.

"Wasn't it a little weird having the alligator turn up that way?" Eli studied the other man as he rubbed his hands by the stove.

"Not really. We get more of them every day in parks, golf courses, even in yards. Though they usually keep their distance . . ." Ranger Dwayne paused.

"What is it?"

"Some boys told one of my men they'd seen someone goading an alligator, seemingly driving it toward the tributary. My man found it hard to believe, since most people shy away from the gators, but he checked it out anyway. He didn't see anything."

"Could someone lure the creature toward the tributary?" Eli's skin crawled with trepidation.

"Yes, it could be done, but not easily. Gators aren't to be fooled with. They can be dangerous at the best of times."

"But someone could direct the creature?"

The ranger nodded. "But why would anyone do that, when they could endanger themselves? Besides, at that time the boy had fallen into the water. What type of hard case would cause peril to a child in such a way?"

"What type, indeed?"

Venus was glad to wash up in warm water and soap. In moments she was clean, her body heat back to normal. When the woman ranger handed her a towel, she smiled. "I'm Venus Wayne." She was taken aback at how the woman's smile faded and her lips tightened. "What is it?"

"My name is Alice Teague. Are you the Venus Wayne who was my cousin's partner?"

"Yes," Venus said faintly. "I came here to see you. A friend of mine, Bahira Massoud . . ."

"Jeremy talked about her and you. He said one of you might come after the ledger." There were tears in Alice Teague's eyes. "I knew there was something wrong when he wanted me to hide it that way. He said you'd come for it if anything happened to him. Jeremy sometimes took too many chances, but he was a good person. He took care of all my mother's medical bills, and he was good to me."

"Believe me, Bahira and I loved him," Venus said, squeezing Alice's arms reassuringly. "I don't know who Jeremy was involved with, but his death might not have been an accident."

Alice nodded. "I wondered about that. Jeremy was so persnickety about details. He always had his car checked, he took care of things."

Venus nodded. "He did. Do you have the ledger?"

Alice nodded. "He wanted me to be so careful with it. I hid it right here in Thursby House, over there." She pointed to the fireplace.

"Here?" Venus looked at the stone chimney. "Jeremy had a little map in Bahira's ledger. It looked like an arrow to a chimney of a house."

Alice nodded. "Let me show you. It's an old hidey-hole that many of the old houses used to have." Alice went over to the old stove and reached down to push against a brick there. When it opened she reached in and brought out a ledger that looked just like the other two. "Here. It's yours. I couldn't make out much of it, anyway." Alice smiled. "I know Jeremy did some wild things, but he had a good heart."

"Yes, he did." Venus stifled a shiver when she took the ledger from Alice. It was as though she'd crossed her Rubicon and, like Caesar, could no longer turn back. She was sure the ledgers had the answers to all her questions . . . and she would have to dig them out and face them. Alice's voice penetrated her thoughts.

"If Jeremy's death wasn't accidental, that means there's a killer on the loose. He or she may be trying to destroy evidence—facts contained in these ledgers."

Venus gazed at the other woman and nodded slowly. "You're probably right."

"In that case, please be careful. We've already lost one life too many."

Venus nodded grimly. Alice put a hand on her shoulder. "I want to go out and check on the boy. Why don't you sit here for a moment? It was a wonderful thing you did today."

"Thank you for this, Alice. I'll let you know what happens."

The ranger nodded and left the room.

Before the door had closed, Venus had the ledger open. Like the other two, this notebook contained inexplicable gaps, as though puzzle pieces were missing.

The best thing to do was talk to Bahira again. Maybe between the two of them they could decode the ledgers—now that they had three of them.

Maybe they could solve Jeremy's riddles. Bahira had always been intuitive about Jeremy. Venus would drive to Epcot and the leather goods store where her friend worked.

Eli! In the excitement of finding the third ledger, Venus had nearly forgotten he was here. Her body warmed anew just thinking of him. She would tell him why she came to Florida. Maybe he could help her decipher the mystery of Jeremy's death.

Venus tapped the third ledger. She would have to be careful. Alice was right. Someone else wanted this information. She shook her head. Jeremy had been her friend, but his love of mystery had sometimes made him too secretive.

The door opened again and Eli stood there. He closed the door behind him and approached her, arms outstretched.

Venus rose to meet him, her hands lacing behind his neck. "I missed you."

"I went a little crazy."

"You were in my mind all the time." Venus pressed her mouth to his neck. His skin was velvet tough under her hands, his crisp hair more erotic to the touch than anything she'd ever known. "Eli." Heart thudding in her chest, she accepted that he was part of her. His very special mystique had a power over her and she could no longer deny it.

"Don't ever leave me again." Eli kissed her neck, his teeth nipping gently at her earlobe.

Venus clutched him. "It didn't seem fair to involve you if Jeremy was entwined in a scam."

Eli leaned back from her. "Tell me the truth. Have you felt that someone, or something, was threatening you?"

Venus gazed back at him long moments before nodding.

"And that's really what made you run down here?"

"Mostly. Someone tried to blackmail me into giving up a ledger that belonged to Jeremy." Venus could feel Eli's body gather itself, the muscles coiling. "I should have told you about it before I came down here."

"Yes, you should have. And I would have come with you." The silken threat in his voice narrowed his eyes.

"You're furious with me."

"Yes, Venus, I am. Did you think I wanted to be wrapped in silk bows while you put yourself in harm's way?"

"No, but—"

"No buts, love. What threatens you is my business and always will be. Whether you take me or leave me, Venus, that won't change."

"I—I wouldn't ever leave for good." Tears clogged her throat. "Don't you know that I couldn't risk getting you involved in this? It's my problem, and I thought I should handle it alone." Her words feathered his mouth as she nuzzled close to him.

"Don't you know that I want to be there for you, to be your support, your buffer?" he whispered.

"I'm a fool, huh?"

"Yes, but you're my fool."

"And you're my fool, Eli."

"Suits me." Some of the tension dissipated—some but not all.

The pressure on her mouth increased until his tongue intruded, jousting with hers.

Thursby House and all of Blue Spring Park faded away as passion took them, fired them, built an aura around them, carried them away.

"I need you . . . so much," Venus whispered. "You've brought new meaning to my life, Eli."

"Have I? Well, you've done the same to me, and I'm going to spend all my time convincing you to marry me. So keep that in mind."

"Eli—"

"Don't cry, darling."

The door opened behind them and someone coughed.

"Ah, Miss Wayne, I don't like to interrupt, but the parents of the boy you saved would like to speak to you."

Shielding Venus with his body, Eli looked over his shoulder. "Thank you, Ranger. We'll be right there."

Venus reached into her shoulder bag to get a tissue and dabbed at her slightly red eyes. Still within the circle of Eli's arms, she slashed pale peach lipstick across her mouth. "I suppose this is the best I can do." She grinned up at her man. "I must look like an unmade bed."

"You're beautiful, Venus Wayne."

"You're beautiful, too, Eli." She laughed when she saw the blood rush to his face. "Hasn't anyone told you you're beautiful before, Eli?"

"Could be. I don't recall. It just never mattered until now."

Venus reached up to touch his cheek. "Do we really have another chance, Eli?"

"Oh, yes, love, we do." He looked down at the black ledger she still clutched in her hand. "Is that part of what brought you here?"

"Yes, I'll tell you all about it, but it's a rather long story." Venus bit her lip. "I know it sounds cryptic, but we don't have the time to go in to it here. It's about Jeremy." She shook her head. "He was complex and intelligent but silly in some ways." She looked at the ledger in her hand. "He hid this here, in Thursby House. There had to be a very good reason for him to compile these crazy notes. And I intend to find out what it all means."

"And you think you will with this ledger?"

Venus frowned. "I'm not sure about anything at this point, but one of our college chums, Bahira Massoud, was also given a ledger. These notes must have been very important for him to go through this cloak-and-dagger type of thing. He wouldn't have felt the need to hide this information away if it wasn't important. Why not a safety deposit box in New York? I think this notebook's some kind of key to the ones that Bahira and I were given. Maybe I'm wrong, but I've got to give it a shot. I'm going back to Epcot to talk to Bahira." She smiled up at him. "Will you go with me?"

"Of course." Eli whistled softly. "And maybe that's the reason someone followed you to Florida."

"Do you mean the bespectacled man? The one who pushed me in front of the cab? I had a funny feeling when I saw him and—"

"Wait a minute, Venus." Eli took hold of her shoulders. "I don't have time to explain it to you now, but believe me, the 'bespectacled man' is not your enemy."

"He isn't?" Venus frowned. "But, Eli, I'm sure he pushed me in front of the cab."

"But the woman who you think saved you could have been the one who tried to kill you. Why else would she have left so abruptly?"

Venus swallowed hard. "A woman! But who? Why?" She shook her head. "I suppose that could be true, but—"

"Not now. We'll talk later." He kissed her hard, vowing to wipe the shadows from her eyes. Eli had his hand at her back as they opened the door, the rise of voices like an assault on their ears.

After they'd talked to the boy and his parents, Venus and Eli left, resuming their discussion of the past twenty-four hours' events.

"And the man with the spectacles drove you here, Eli? How is he getting back?"

"He'll drive. He said he was going to look around, but I imagine he was out of the park long before us."

Venus shot a quick look at him. "I can't believe you're here."

Eli slouched in his seat, watching her. "Believe it, Venus. I'm going to be with you all the way."

She nodded. Happiness spread through her like warm syrup, coating her with the security and serenity that being with Eli always brought. She bit her lip on a sigh.

Eli touched her arm gently. "Tell me what you're thinking."

"I was remembering how *Forbes* magazine described you as the wrestler of the business world, always ready to come out of your corner. Today you wrestled an alligator." Even though she tried to laugh, her body shuddered.

"I was close to him, but the rangers got him before he got to me. Remember that, darling."

She nodded, but she wouldn't forget how once more Eli had stepped between her and death.

"Tell me about your friend Bahira."

Venus sighed. "She is a dear college acquaintance from Morocco. She was close to Jeremy, too. In fact, she feels that his death was not an accident."

Eli gave her a steely gaze and moved fractionally closer, his hand moving to her knee.

Venus felt comforted by his touch. He was able to dissipate the blackness just by being near. She wanted to be in bed with him, body to body, mouth to mouth.

"Why did your face just turn red?" he asked. "I hope it's what I've been thinking. We haven't made love in ages. Shall we go back to the suite I have at the Royal Palm?"

Venus smiled at him regretfully. "We can go there to shower and change, but I have to see Bahira."

Eli grimaced. "Damned if I won't get this whole mess ironed out in a hurry. We need to be together without so much between us."

"Yes," she agreed wholeheartedly.

"Venus, love, we are going to spend New Year's Eve in each other's arms, no matter what city we're in."

"I'd like that."

"Let's get to Epcot and settle the business of the ledgers quickly."

Venus shook her head. "I wonder if I'll ever fully understand Jeremy now."

"I think you knew him as well as anyone, Venus. But it sounds as if Jeremy flirted with the dark side of life."

"Yeah, I guess he did. The sooner I get those three ledgers together, the sooner we can decipher Jeremy's intentions . . . maybe. There's nothing salvageable for Teague and Wayne, that's for sure, but I still want to know what happened when he took the turn that forced him over the edge on the bull market." Venus bit her lip. "And I'd like to know who was in on it with him. Jeremy was imaginative, but I don't think he would have tackled anything too intricate unless someone was urging him."

"Or goading him." Eli looked thoughtful. "He had to have some pretty heavy friends to get in as deep as he seems to have done."

The hotel suite was large and had two bathrooms. After they'd showered and dressed, they faced each other in the sitting room.

"You look ten years old in that outfit." Eli smiled at her and bent to kiss her lightly.

Venus's arms slipped around his waist. "I wish we could stay here."

"But we've got to get this damned thing settled." He kissed the tip of her nose. "When this is over, we're going to spend a week in bed."

"Mind boggling."

"Let's go, temptress."

This time Eli drove Bahira's truck. Venus sat close to him, her hand on his thigh, during the short drive. After they parked the truck, they hurried to the turnstiles at the entrance to Epcot.

"Eli, how did you find me so fast?"

"The bespectacled man, of course."

Venus wrinkled her nose, looking puzzled.

"Uncle Dismas has been acting on his flawless instincts. After the shooting incident he hired private investigators to follow both of us. Spider has been on your tail ever since.

Venus laughed. "*Spider?* Now I know we're getting close to the underworld. Thank God for Dismas's instincts."

Eli nodded, pulling her closer.

Flowers and foil balloons seemed to swirl around them. "I hadn't realized this was such a pretty place. I hadn't looked at it when I was here earlier," Venus said.

"Me, either. I was too busy looking for you." Eli murmured. He leaned down, oblivious to the crowds streaming around them. "I love you."

Trembling, she reached up and pulled his hard mouth to her own. The kiss was a gentle covenant. "And I love you."

In Venus's eyes Epcot had a new shimmer and glint to it that had nothing to do with the Christmas decorations that abounded. Even the dark side of Jeremy's life couldn't intrude on the beautiful world Eli had created for her.

Watching the couple board the boat from the shelter of an ice cream kiosk along the edge of the lake, he burned with anger.

The alligator could have finished the job, cleanly, quickly, and pretty little Venus would have been no more. It was such a damned rotten quirk of fate that the rangers were so near to the scene.

Next time there would be no mistakes.

Chapter Eight

Venus tried to ignore a pang of worry. Eli could suffer from the mistakes Jeremy had made. His board of directors was a thorn in his side already. What would their reaction be when Jeremy's vagaries came to light? The CEO at Weldon-Tate was seeing the former partner of a criminal! Venus squeezed her eyes shut.

When they debarked, Venus gestured toward the Tangiers Traders sign. "Bahira's a salesperson in leather goods."

"Let's go."

Venus laughed when he pulled her into a trot.

They walked into the small store at the front of the Moroccan Showcase, sniffing the pungent and pleasing smell of the leather.

Eli grinned at her as he kissed her lightly on the cheek. "I can't resist. My imagination has you decked out in one of those skimpy beaded dresses on the wall . . . and nothing else."

Venus was out of breath, off-balance, off the mark as she was every time Eli kissed her. She didn't move out of his arms, wanting the touch of his body. Sighing, she leaned closer. She would always need him.

"Whew, it's heating up in here. I take it this is the one who's so important, Venus." Bahira appeared from the back room, smiling, but the tension was evident in her lovely face.

"I found another ledger," Venus announced.

"You did? Wow! What does it say?"

"I haven't had time to look at it." Venus introduced Eli to Bahira.

"You're welcome to come to Manhattan any time and visit us." Eli smiled.

"Thanks, I will."

While the two of them exchanged pleasantries, Venus looked up at Eli. With Eli in charge, the world could be dealt with and wrestled to the ground.

Life was going to be wonderful with him ... Venus stopped in her tracks. She was picturing her future with Eli. Would there be children? Sturdy little boys with strong chins and a determined gleam in their eyes, red-haired girls who would captivate all? And the boys would have streaky dark blond hair and emerald-green eyes.

"Venus? What are you thinking, darling?"

"Good thoughts," she answered breathily, turning to Bahira. "Is there some place we could go that's private? I need your help with this."

Bahira nodded. "Whoops. I have a customer, but I'll be with you in a minute."

A figure loomed outside the window of the shop, watching ... waiting. Pretty little Venus Wayne! She'd been an irritant from the start. She had to be handled.

Why had she returned to the Moroccan Showcase with Weldon-Tate? What did she know? Covering all the bases was the way to success. Knowing what the enemy knew was the greatest protection. Damn Jeremy Teague and his penchant for record keeping!

What were they doing in there? It would be better if Weldon-Tate wasn't here.

Eli watched her as she opened her bag and took out the three ledgers. "You want some time to go over them alone with Bahira?" he asked.

"Actually, I have ambivalent feelings now. I want to know . . . but I'm frightened of the truth."

"I don't want any more secrets between us, Venus. Why don't I go over the ledgers with you?" He touched a curling strand of her silken red hair that had fallen forward on her face, his fingers lingering on her cheek.

Venus lifted her hand and placed it over his. "I'd like that, more than you know, but I think I should look at them by myself the first time. I think I might get better vibrations." She touched his cheek. "And I don't want you to be hurt by something that has nothing to do with you."

"If it's about you, I'm not only interested, I'm involved. I thought we went through all that."

Venus nodded heavily and swiped at her tear-dampened cheeks. "I suppose I should stop fighting you, Eli Weldon-Tate."

"That would be smart."

"I'm smart . . . sometimes." Venus stared up at him, tears burning in her eyes.

"Don't cry." Eli hugged her. "You feel so good, love."

Venus's chuckle vibrated against his chest. Eli laughed with her, but it didn't lessen the ever-present tension. A black shadow had hovered over them since that first day in the lobby when the sniper had fired at her. Loving her, cherishing her, Eli knew they were intrinsically tied together for life. But now he had to get to the bottom of this. What was threatening her—and why?

He knew enough about security at Weldon-Tate to surmise that it was more than adequate here at Epcot. That knowledge brought him a measure of comfort.

Bahira grimaced at them as she was forced to wait on another customer.

"We'll wait outside," Eli called to her as he led Venus toward the door. He looked down at her in the sunshine. If anyone had told him even three months ago that a lissome lady with red-gold hair and violet eyes would take over his life and direct his every emotion, he would have scoffed. Now here was Venus!

Leaving her alone was anathema to him. The thought that there could be unfriendly eyes watching her made his skin crawl, even though he knew feeling threatened in the middle of an amusement park was irrational. It took all his strength to smile at her. All he wanted to do was scoop her up and take the next plane to a deserted island. A lifetime alone with her wouldn't be enough.

The figure watched them stroll out of the leather goods shop, hand in hand.

There was no way to know what they said as they stood there, unaware that they were being studied like specimens under a microscope. The concourse was wide and filled with people, a perfect cover.

Although the acid of hate gnawed away at his innards, he found a rather macabre humor in the situation. Did pretty little Venus Wayne lead a charmed life? It would seem so. Yet she didn't know she was being stalked.

Not even the very shrewd Eli Weldon-Tate was aware that a loaded gun was poised to put a hole in the back of his neck. Would that be the thing to do? Finish them off here and now in the crowd? Who would notice? The throngs had grown. People were everywhere, moving in every direction. Not a bad idea. Maybe it would be better to wait until they were out on the concourse. Then duck down with the crowd, get to the lake, drop the gun in there. Great plan!

Not that it would have been such a bad thing if the alligator had gotten Weldon-Tate . . . or Wayne . . . or both. Damn! If only it hadn't taken so long to get the alligator into the tributary. It would have solved the problems. But there was no need to repine. The original idea had been to take care of the Wayne woman first, then Weldon-Tate. Getting them together might be neater.

Would they spot his disguise? Probably not. Getting closer and listening to their conversation could be helpful.

A girl, passing by, almost spilled ice cream on his costume. "Hey, watch where you're going!"

The little girl stared upward. "You're an awfully crabby Pluto. Mickey was nicer."

"Merry Christmas," he said, patting the child's head.

Best not to incite the little darlings. Children were a bore, but they could be troublesome as well. No need for that.

Eli found it difficult to leave Venus, even though he wouldn't be far away. "All right. I'll wait for you out here. Maybe I'll go over to France and have a glass of wine." Eli indicated the outdoor café of the showcase next to Morocco.

"I'll look for you around here," Venus promised. "It won't take long. Who knows? We may need you to help us interpret Jeremy's hen scratchings."

Eli leaned down, rubbing his lips across hers before kissing her deeply. "I'll be waiting, lady mine."

Out of breath, Venus could only nod.

Eli watched her walk out of sight, loving the sway of her body, the fluid motion of arms and legs. Tall, slender, beautiful, and she was his to cherish. "Whoops, pardon me." Eli turned around to see who he'd bumped into. "Sorry, Pluto."

The character nodded stiffly and backed away awkwardly.

Eli didn't think the imitation of Pluto was that good. No doubt it was a university student trying to earn money, maybe one who'd never seen Pluto in the movies when he was a kid.

Shrugging, Eli meandered to the café, took a seat facing the Moroccan Showcase, and signaled for a waiter.

Venus re-entered the leather goods store and noted that her friend was still busy. How lovely and delicate the diminutive Bahira looked in her native clothing.

Bahira looked up and saw her at once, smiling and beckoning her closer. She was just saying good-bye to a customer.

Setting her bag on a counter in the back of the shop, Venus opened up each notebook. Both women leaned over them, studying them intently.

Bahira shook her head. "I'm afraid I'm not much help. We need more time with this. And the shop is so busy today. Why don't you put the first two side by side and ... Ah, yes, sir, that's genuine Moroccan leather. There are others behind you." Bahira winked at Venus, then went to assist the customer.

Venus leaned against the terra-cotta wall and turned her attention to the notebook found at Blue Spring Park. It was tough going. Again she had the feeling that studying all three notebooks together would reveal what Jeremy was trying to say.

When she finally took note of a prickling sense of discomfort, she straightened. Danger! Venus looked up and gazed around her. Someone was watching her.

It was Pluto, but his stare was so fixed. Unable to see Bahira now, Venus felt alone and isolated. As she moved, so did Pluto—right toward her. "Hi."

Pluto didn't answer but took another step toward her, crowding her, hemming her into the corner of the shop.

"Mommy! Look! Hi, Pluto."

Pluto turned his head, obviously annoyed.

Venus blessed the child. Shoving the ledgers into her bag, she moved sideways through the bazaar, toward the door. When she glanced over her shoulder, Pluto was behind her, a small group of people in between them.

Breaking into a run, panic rising in her throat, she stumbled pell-mell through a door to a large area, coming to a skidding stop. Where to go?

"There's nothing more to see here, Nathaniel," the child's mother said. "Come along and we'll go to the China area."

The voices penetrated Venus's churning mind. She turned toward the boy and his mother, who were part of a large tour group of adults with cameras and children with bright foil balloons.

"But I like it here," the boy said to his long-suffering parent. "I want to play with Pluto."

Venus bit her lip. This Pluto was trouble—for

her and any unsuspecting kid who thought the person in the costume was legitimate. She had to think fast!

A tiny Asian girl smiled at Venus, revealing two pearly front teeth. Could Venus persuade this group to follow her? She had to give it a shot. It was the only way to steer herself and these kids clear of the menacing Pluto.

"Ah, ladies and gentlemen, boys and girls, why don't you try the Japan Showcase? I'm going there right now," Venus said breathily, moving into the center of the group. "If you'll just follow me, I can guarantee you won't be disappointed with the wonders of the Orient!"

A few of the people looked at her inquisitively.

"Are you a tour guide?" one woman asked.

"I'd be delighted to show you anything you're interested in," Venus answered, dodging the question and flashing a bright smile at the group.

"Do you hear that, Nathaniel?"

"I don't care. I like it here."

"You'll like Japan." Venus could see Pluto closing in on them. She took hold of the boy's hand. "Let me help you, dear."

Young Nathaniel eyed her warily, but when the Asian girl came over and grabbed Venus's other hand, the boy seemed to warm up.

"Adorable, isn't he?" Venus remarked to the bemused mother as she swept by her, the children in tow.

"Do you like your work?" the mother queried, hurrying to keep up.

"You could say that," Venus muttered, looking around for Pluto.

At last! They were outside the Moroccan bazaar! Glancing once behind her, Venus saw the edge of the Pluto costume. Who was behind the mask? The vision of the incident with the taxi loomed in her mind. Had the woman pushed her? Eli had said the bespectacled man was a detective named Spider. Was there a woman in the Pluto suit? Then she saw Pluto coming toward the group.

There was no escaping the pursuer now!

Striding right up to the character, Venus reached over and gave a yank on his tail. "Now, Pluto," she exclaimed in a loud voice so that the whole crowd could hear. "You know you're not supposed to be on this side of the park!"

The character froze with its hands on its hips as some of the children giggled in anticipation of a show.

"Now shoo!" Venus exclaimed. "Get back to Disney World before you miss the parade—or there'll be no supper for you!"

Pluto hesitated for a minute, then backed away in defeat. A moment later, the crowd roared with laughter, politely clapping for Venus and Pluto.

As Venus bowed demurely, her thoughts flashed to Eli. He would be at the French café. Now that Pluto was scared off, she could leave these people to their own devices.

"Take care, Nathaniel. I have to run."

"Hey, wait!" the boy insisted. "I thought you were taking us to Japan!"

"Come, Nathaniel." The boy's mother grabbed his arm. "Let the nice lady get back to work."

"Have a wonderful day," Venus called as she waved to the crowd. The cheerful waves and farewells from the children gave her a surge of pride. She'd done the right thing, scaring Pluto away from them. Turning away, Venus sprinted toward the café, finally spotting Eli. At once as he rose to his feet, his face twisted in confusion.

Eli dropped some money on the table and, vaulting over a chair in his path, ran onto the concourse, his gaze shooting left and right. What had put the trepidation in Venus's eyes?

"Eli! Don't go that way."

"What is it?" He pulled her into his arms, looking over his head. "Is something wrong?"

"Yes ... no. I don't know. Maybe it was my imagination, but ..."

Eli felt her body tremble. "Easy does it. Tell me what happened. Come on over here. I'm going to buy you some wine and cheese. You need to catch your breath and relax, then you can tell me what frightened you." Eli took her arm, keeping her close to his side as he led her to a table.

Ignoring the few curious stares turned their way, Eli signaled for the waiter. "Bring a glass of Paul Bocuse Vin Rouge for the lady, please."

Venus kept her hands clasped in her lap until the waiter left. She tried to smile when Eli looked back at her. "I came running right to you."

He lifted her hand, smiling lazily, masking his anger and fear. "You did the right thing."

"Eli, maybe I was stupid."

"Tell me."

"I thought ... thought I was being stalked by Pluto," Venus said in a rush. "It sounds silly. What could he have done, anyway? I really had nothing to fear with so many people around, but there are so many children here ..." She had been terrified, quite sure that the person in the Pluto costume was ready, willing, and able to hurt someone if given the chance. No amount of rationalization could make that feeling go away. People were killed in crowds all the time, and the perpetrators were never caught. This Pluto-dressed person could have managed to do the same. Venus shuddered.

"Pluto?" Eli rose to his feet, scanning the crowds of people milling along the concourse. "That character bumped into me. I thought he was a poor imitation of Disney's dream."

"You believe me?"

Eli frowned at her. "Of course I believe you . . . and I'm getting you out of Florida this afternoon." Eli resumed his seat, taking her hand in his. "Someone wants you badly. Someone besides me—and for a very different reason. I'm going to keep you safe."

Venus nodded. "And I'm not letting anyone get to you, either."

"Good." Eli grinned and leaned forward to give her a quick kiss.

"Your wine, Mademoiselle," the waiter announced woodenly.

Eli leaned back slowly. "Drink that, then we'll tell Bahira that we're leaving. I also want to report this to Security. They should be informed of this impostor."

Venus nodded, sipping the wine, her shaking hands gripping the glass with two hands.

Once again pretty little Venus Wayne had run to Eli Weldon-Tate, her savior. Frustrating! Infuriating!

The woman had finely honed instincts for self-preservation. The admiration was grudging. Being foiled again was a bitter pill to swallow. That notebook she'd been holding was very like the ones that Jeremy Teague used to make copious notes in, detail after detail. Such habits can be dangerous in a colleague. How many of the damned things had he filled? Jeremy Teague had been too smart. Damn Jeremy for keeping a back-up file!

The demise of Venus Wayne and Eli Weldon-

Tate now took on new meaning. Killing one without the other was no good; they were too hooked on each other. Too much information had been shared between them.

He'd already discarded the Pluto suit in a trash can. But donning the gray wig had proved to be a little more involved. There were people everywhere in Epcot. Privacy was hard to find.

He frowned at the couple sitting in the outdoor café. Weldon-Tate seemed to have eyes in the back of his head, glancing at everyone and everything. He was too damned smart.

Staying any longer in Florida could be dangerous. Better to get back to the relative anonymity of New York . . . that very day.

Eli was angrier than he'd ever been in his life, but he spoke gently to the woman at his side. "We're going home today, Venus, and we won't be parted again."

"I need to hear that." Venus couldn't quite stem the fear that still filled her.

Pluto, whoever that was, had wanted to kill her.

Now that she was somewhat calmer, she accepted that with frightening certainty. Was it all tied together? The sniper, the taxi incident, the near-miss in the garage, the alligator? Did they all have something to do with Jeremy's ledgers? And what about Benedict's cryptic warning? Where did that fit in?

"You're thinking about what happened, aren't you?" Eli put his arm around her as they took a bus back to the Royal Palm.

"I can't help it. Too many coincidences."

"I agree. I know that you'll have a hard time thinking of anything else. But please believe I intend to get to the bottom of this, to drive this danger out of your life."

"I know you'll try . . . but this person seems to know what we're thinking, Eli. Like an evil spirit or something." Venus closed her eyes and pushed her face into his shoulder. "I sound like a fool."

"You've been damned brave." Eli kissed her hair. He would keep her safe.

"Who do you think is following us, Eli?"

He squeezed her hand as the bus turned in the curving drive to the Royal Plaza. "At the moment, all I know is that he or she is a threat to you."

"Do you think Disney World Security will turn up anything?"

Eli shrugged as he rose to his feet and led her from the bus. "I don't know, but I'm going to keep in touch with them."

Venus was momentarily diverted by the antics of the cockateels in the lobby. They were a wistful reminder of her former pet. "Don't they try to escape? They aren't caged."

"Their wings are clipped and they are in an environment they seem to enjoy. They certainly have enough doting fans." Eli took her arm and led her to the elevator, which sped them to the top floor.

Venus breathed a sigh of relief once they were in the suite. "It's lovely here. The rooms are so large . . . and what a view from the balcony." She whirled to face him. "Do you think the showers are large enough for two? The shower I took earlier was refreshing, but something was missing . . ."

Eli's heart missed a beat at the reckless glitter in her eyes. He knew that fear still lingered inside her, but she'd tamped it down, put it into a niche inside her brain. His lady had guts and he respected that, but he wished, in a way, that she wasn't quite so brave. A little cowardice might make her come to him with all of her problems.

"Something was missing from mine, too," he drawled, not even trying to stem the passion that was coursing through his body. "Let's take a shower the way a shower was meant to be taken!"

"Well, what are we waiting for?"

"Nothing." Eli saw the desperation behind her smile. "Let me undress you, ma'am."

"Thank you.'

"And you can do the same for me," he murmured.

"I will." The smile left her face. "I need you, Eli."

"I know, darling. And I need you." He knew Venus hadn't lost her fears and was trying to forget them for a time. And he was damn well going to try to help her do that.

"Lucky we're here."

Eli kissed her lopsided smile, his mouth moving gently over hers. "I will always be here for you, Venus."

"Love me, Eli."

He swept her up into his arms, carrying her into one of the capacious bathrooms and stripping the clothes from her body, scattering them on the vanity that stretched along one wall. Holding her in one arm, he reached into the shower cubicle that was separate from the large tub with the two steps leading up to it.

Under the pulsating water, Eli laved her with fragrant soap and then shampooed her hair.

"My turn," Venus said huskily as his hands performed magic on her skin.

In slow, erotic motions they were washed, words seeming unnecessary as their hands spoke for them.

"I love kissing your breasts, darling. You're so beautiful." Eli took one pink tip into his mouth, forcing the nipple into pebble hardness, then he ministered to the other one.

"Eli!" A groan of delight was torn from Venus as she took his head into her hands, the feel of that lightly stubbled chin erotic in the extreme.

"Should I shave, darling?" His eyes, slumberous from loving her, stared into hers.

"You feel wonderful."

Eli lifted her out of the shower, taking a liquid emollient and patting it over her body. "Damn, I shouldn't do this. I've never been so aroused in my life. You have the power, Venus Wayne."

She put some of the fragrant oil in her hand and began to massage him with it.

"You're crazy, lady." Eli lifted her high into his arms, his hands trembling. "It's as though I've never loved anyone but you . . . maybe I haven't."

Venus nodded. She coiled her arms around his neck and pressed her mouth to his throat. Again she fantasized about spending a lifetime with Eli, bearing his children. The thought made her heart beat out of rhythm.

When Eli placed her on the bed, she pulled him down with her, loath to release him. "Love me, Eli."

"I've thought of doing nothing else since our first meeting. I need you, Venus. Stay with me."

She gasped when she felt his mouth map every pore of her skin, touch every indentation, caress every curve.

His tongue touched her navel in a thrusting motion that shivered through her. As he moved lower, her body arched in expectation of the ultimate caress. His mouth moved over her, searing her in the passion of sensuous love. "I want you, Venus, I always will."

"Eli!" Words spilled from Venus's mind, but her trembling lips wouldn't form them. Grasping him, she pulled him up so that their mouths met in a fiery kiss.

In gentle fierceness, he took her, her body closing around him like a velvet prison, eliciting gasps of ecstasy from him.

Slowly his thrusts increased, her rhythm building to his. Alone in their aura they left the planet, spinning out into space, holding each other, becoming one in an explosion of happiness.

Shaken, Eli held her, soothing her body with kisses and words of love. "It was wonderful. I love you, Venus."

"And I love you." Shocked, she stared up at him. "How did that happen?"

Eli chuckled. "Marry me, and I'll spend a lifetime explaining it."

Joy radiated through her, then she came down with a thump. How could she marry anyone, especially Eli? Someone considered her a threat, hated her enough to make attempts on her life.

Wasn't it bad enough that she had involved Eli so much already? She didn't have the right to endanger him. Besides, she couldn't bear it if anything happened to him. She reached up and touched his face. He was the most precious part of her life.

"Venus? What is it? You're not planning on trying to leave me again, are you?"

She shook her head. "I should, but I can't . . . However, I don't want to think of marriage right now, Eli. I need time." She winced at the harsh twisting of his features, black lightning. "Will you give me that time?"

"Dammit, Venus, I . . ." he hesitated. "Yes, I'll give you that time." Eli rolled out of bed, walking to the window, staring out into the fading Florida sunshine.

Venus studied his nude form. Was there ever a man so beautiful? His buttocks were curved and hard muscled as were his long legs. His waist opened upward to a strong back and wide shoulders. "Do you know I love you, really love you, Eli?"

"What?" He seemed distracted, far away. "Yes, I know that." His colorless voice telegraphed his anger to her.

Venus sighed.

He swung around to face her. "I'll call the airport about our flight."

"I'd better dampen my hair again. It's all flyaway," Venus said haltingly.

"But still lovely," Eli drawled, his smile tight. "I'll use the phone in the living room."

Venus felt chilled when she went into the shower again to dampen her hair. Because she was so cold she decided to stand under the hot water, but the coldness inside her didn't dissipate.

It hurt so much to be at odds with Eli when all she wanted to do was curl up in his arms for a century.

They hurriedly dressed and packed, leaving the suite in a rush.

In the lobby, Eli looked out the glass doors. "There's Spider."

Venus adjusted her shoulder bag and went out as a shiny black limousine pulled up to the front of the hotel. Her mouth dropped when a man got out of the car and took her bag. The bespectacled man! "It's—it's—"

Eli put his arm around her. "I told you. It's Spider."

"Even his hat is the same," she muttered.

"Dismas trusts him implicitly. He hired Spider fresh out of Attica."

"Delightful," she murmured, scrambling into the car on her own before Spider could open her door.

Leaning forward, she peeked at their unusual driver, then sat back when she noticed his eyes on her in the rearview mirror.

Eli caught her as Spider screeched away from the curb and she was thrown sideways. "I told him to hurry or we wouldn't make our flight." Eli kissed her hair.

Venus looked up with a relieved smile.

"Don't misinterpret the caress, darling. I love you, but I'm still damned furious with you," Eli told her silkily. "I wish you would agree to marry me."

She stared up at him for a moment. How could she describe her fears of marriage? She could never be the kind of wife Eli needed—an attractive companion who could play hostess at parties and charity functions. After a taste of Wall Street, Venus couldn't settle for a sedate home life. But it seemed so selfish of her! "You must be hell in a boardroom," she finally murmured.

"I am . . . and I don't like losing. Keep that in mind."

What would Venus Wayne and Eli Weldon-Tate do if they had an inkling that "Pluto" was on the same plane winging them back to chilly Manhattan?

It was too good to be true! The three of them would be getting out of the plane together to finish out the year with a bang, so to speak. There were only a few days of this year left, but a lot could happen in a few days. The deaths of Venus Wayne and Eli Weldon-Tate, for instance. What a wonderful prospect! So far his luck was holding. With a few smart moves, all would go well. There would be no questions and a great deal of money would be in "Pluto's" hands.

Those ledgers were the irritating factor here. How many were there? Damn Jeremy Teague! Curse his soul. Killing him again would be a pleasure.

Manhattan was aglitter in the early evening, the Christmas lights still beckoning brightly.

"A new year is coming," Venus offered tentatively.

"And I've made a resolution: You won't ever get away from me again."

"I don't want to leave you, Eli. You know that. Living together is in our future. Couldn't we just enjoy that for a while?" Even if she could overcome her fear of marriage, Venus couldn't commit herself to Eli when so much of her life was unresolved.

"Do you have doubts about our relationship? Things that are keeping you from marriage?"

Venus opened her mouth and shut it again before she answered. "Why can't we just accept the status quo, Eli?"

"Because you are trying to push me out of your life in a stupid, inane attempt to protect me, and I won't have it."

After the plane had taxied up to the jetway and the two-bell signal sounded, Eli rose to his feet. He eased the carry-on luggage into position and gestured for Venus to precede him.

"My car is being brought around to the entrance. I called ahead from Orlando."

"Money bags," Venus muttered, running to catch

up with him. "Don't we have to get the other luggage?"

"It will be taken care of."

"Mogul."

"Was that *mongrel* or *mogul*?"

"Take your pick." Chin high, Venus stepped through the automatic doors to the outside. At once the cold north air hit her and she began shivering.

When the car pulled up, Venus climbed in and snuggled into the plush upholstery of the Rolls-Royce. Having forgotten to put on the jacket she'd been carrying, she was chilled. Shrugging into it now, she watched as Eli came around the hood of the car and slipped behind the wheel. "Are we going right to the apartment?" she asked.

"Had you another destination in mind?"

"No. But we do have to eat . . ."

Eli laughed. "I'm glad all this excitement hasn't curbed your appetite." Remembering their heated discussion only moments earlier, he added, "All right, but let's call a truce. I don't want us to fight anymore."

"Me, either."

"What would you say to some broiled lobster tail and champagne for two? Sort of an early New Year's celebration."

"Whoopee!" Venus laughed out loud, feeling the first real lightness of spirit all day.

Eli reached across the seat and pulled her close to him. "Happy New Year, lady mine."

Chapter Nine

Venus looked out the window of her office, staring at the January gloom of Manhattan. At least the days were getting longer. She really didn't mind the gray days or the mounds of snow that had collected on the city streets. She liked snow and enjoyed skiing, and, counter to all the theories, she was very productive on slate-colored days. All should have been well, but Venus was uneasy.

She still hadn't solved any of the mysteries surrounding Jeremy, nor did she know who wanted the ledgers badly enough to blackmail—or kill—her.

And there was also Eli. Every day, in subtle but sweet ways, he asked for a deeper love, a commitment she wasn't ready to give. His bland looks didn't fool her. Under that facade, his megapower was churning. Diabolical man! He'd warned Venus that his pursuit would be relentless, but she'd had no idea of the intense magnetism he possessed.

Oh, they made love every night—wondrous, sizzling, passionate love—but Venus still held back from Eli, and he was beginning to notice.

That morning when they were about to leave for work, he'd broached the subject.

"You seem to be brooding about something. Care to talk about it?"

"Brooding?" Distracted, Venus glanced at her watch. "I have an early meeting. We'd better leave. Ready?"

She knew she was driving him crazy. Each night they would sit together and talk about anything and everything, but if he asked what was troubling her, she changed the subject. Though he smiled, there was a steely glitter in his gaze that telegraphed his determination to win her over.

When they ate breakfast together, she would catch his watchful gaze on her. At lunch his stare was no less intense. In the evenings it was easier because by then they desired each other so much that nothing got in the way of their passions—not friends, not discussion.

Once, in the middle of an embrace, naked body to naked body, he'd pulled back from her, hair mussed, eyes glazed with desire. "Damn you, Venus, you're a witch."

Still caught in the magical ecstasy that their lovemaking generated, she'd blinked up at him. "What does that mean, Eli?"

"I love you, dammit." Then he'd covered her surprised laughter with his mouth.

She'd expected roughness when he thrust into her, but, as always, she had gotten the gentle intensity that drove her wild. Her body arched into his, taking him, wanting all of him, needing him desperately.

Venus had never expected to be so captivated physically and spiritually by one person. He filled her world. Giving in and marrying him would be so easy, so right, so wonderful . . . but what then? Would her personal stalker turn to Eli? Hurt him? Kill him?

And would their marriage be the blessed union

it was supposed to be? Venus had her doubts. She loved Eli with all her heart, but she wasn't sure she was woman enough to be his wife. Old childhood fears as familiar as her own shadow rose up to haunt her as she stared out at the stark Manhattan skyline. Orphaned at a young age, Venus never knew her mother. She grew up without a family, without any role models. All her knowledge of relationships had come later in life, from books, movies, and friends.

Shuddering, she shook her head, trying to clear her mind of its turmoil. Now, as she looked out the floor-to-ceiling windows, she found no easy answers. Her face touched the chill glass and she flinched.

Eli was the core of her life. There was no way to evade that truth. How long could she hide her heart from him?

And yet, in his own way, Eli was equally stubborn. He refused to take precautions for his own well-being, but he hovered over Venus like a mother hen. And they'd quarreled more than once about the topic.

"Your argument has no merit, Venus. No one is after me."

"You don't know that for sure, do you?"

"I'm sure enough," Eli had answered smoothly.

"You think it's all right to be so cavalier about yourself, do you? You're not Superman. Someone could get to you." Fear and anger warred inside her at the thought. "You have no right to be so careless."

"You know damn well I'm not foolhardy."

Her chin went higher. "I know you're too offhand about danger to yourself. What makes you so positive you weren't the target of the gunman that first day in the lobby?"

"Two things. First, Dismas has had a man on me like a blanket; even before I met you I was being watched. Second, the other near misses always involved you."

"You were there at times, too."

"Sometimes, but you were always the target." Eli hauled her close to his chest, keeping her hands imprisoned between them. "That fiery temper of yours matches your hair. I'll have to learn to bob and weave a little better." He shook his head, a reluctant smile touching his mouth.

"Yes. Damn you, Eli, for being so careless about yourself." Venus's eyes fluttered shut when his hands whirled over her back and hips in a tender massage. Where did his power come from? The stars? The moon? "I should belt you in the jaw."

"Can't. I have your hands trapped between us," Eli muttered. "I should paddle you." His mouth moved down her cheek.

"I'll paddle you back."

"It wouldn't work as a punishment, anyway. Touching you always excites me too much." He touched his lips to her cheek. "Any children we might have should be trained for the boxing ring. No sense wasting such feisty spirits."

Venus felt her blood congeal. "Children? Don't be silly."

"I'm not. Don't you want to be the mother of my children? I'd love to start a family with you, Venus," he whispered.

She tensed, trying to fight the maternal instincts that tugged at her heart. "You're being silly."

"Am I? And would that be so terrible?" he asked with a warm look. When he noticed the strain on her face, he backed off. "We'll table the discussion, then. Shall we go to bed?"

"Without dessert?"

"You're my dessert, angel. I'll start at your toes and nibble my way to your lips. Along the way there should be quite a few exciting . . . bites."

Eli's sensuous voice ran over her skin like a particularly sexy caress, turning her limbs to gelatin. "I think I'm going to have you registered with the FBI," she muttered, "as a very lethal weapon."

For hours they had loved each other, kissing and holding each other with passion's clasp. The night had not been long enough.

Venus sighed at the memory and turned away from the window. All her fears and doubts couldn't dull the luster of the love they shared. Last night had been as explosive, as exciting, as wonderful as all the other times they'd had together.

Her world had taken on a glow since Eli had come into her life. Used to being on her own after the death of her beloved grandmother, she'd developed self-confidence, a belief in herself that not even the debacle with Jeremy and their firm had totally damaged.

Yet, since she'd met Eli, there was more. It wasn't recklessness exactly, but she had the swashbuckling surety that she could deal with the fears that assailed her, that she could go head to head with the "stalker" and come out a winner.

If only all the wondering was over! Why didn't her enemy show himself? Tackling life day by day, one step at a time, still left so much in limbo. Damn the phantom person who was putting her life in a holding pattern.

Venus came out of her reverie, back to the reality of her work in the Weldon-Tate Building.

Putting her fingers up to her forehead as though the gesture could push the memories of that evening to the back of her mind, she tried to concentrate on what she had to do.

There were so many things to tackle that day. First and foremost was the disk that had disappeared from her locked drawer. When she'd returned from Florida, it had been one of the things she'd looked for at once, but she hadn't found it.

Shaking her head, she went back and sat down at her desk, going through the drawers once more, operating on the theory that the disk could have dropped behind something. No luck.

Glancing at her watch, she noticed that she had thirty minutes until her lunch hour was over. Eli was attending a luncheon with the board of directors, and she missed him. Settling for an apple and a glass of milk at her desk rather than going down to the well-stocked restaurant for the Weldon-Tate employees, she'd searched for the lost disk . . . when she wasn't thinking of Eli.

She decided to use this time to go over Jeremy's ledgers again. Maybe an entry would catch her eye; she might notice something she'd overlooked. Venus couldn't give up on them. Jeremy had put too much effort into writing them.

Venus reached for her bag and removed the three ledgers that she always kept with her, toting them to work and home again. Eli kept telling her that it was wiser to keep them in the safe at the apartment.

He had helped her scrutinize the ledgers, and they had come up with some very interesting names that he was checking. The columns of figures had begun to make some sense, but there was still a great deal they didn't know.

Venus vowed that no matter how long it took, she would decipher Jeremy's message.

A sudden prickling sense of survival compelled her to close the door to the outer corridor and lock it. Then, placing the three ledgers side by side, she opened each of them to the first page and scanned each one. Gobbledygook! First she read one page, then another, then the last. Nothing. What sort of code was Jeremy using? Would she ever know?

She was leaning forward, her folded arms across the ledgers, when she noticed that a few words were underlined on each page. Maybe that was a key to something. Picking up her pen, she wrote down each word. More gibberish. On impulse she picked up the ledger that Jeremy had designated as hers and switched its place. That didn't seem to make much difference, but Venus noticed that there was some sense between hers and Bahira's.

Shifting the three open ledgers like chess pieces so that hers was first, Bahira's second, and the Thursby House ledger third, Venus took up her pen again, only to throw it down almost at once as words with meaning jumped right out at her.

The underlined words now made sense, connecting up into a very clear message.

<u>IN CASE OF MY DEATH, THIS WILL GIVE THE ANSWERS TO THE QUESTIONS THAT MIGHT ARISE. MY DEATH WILL NOT HAVE BEEN ACCIDENTAL.</u>

Venus gasped and leaned back in her chair, the flat of her hands covering the condemning words. It couldn't be! Faulty brakes had caused the accident. Jeremy hadn't made the turn because he'd been driving too fast . . . right through the guardrail into the churning Fishkill River. He'd combined a business trip upstate with the pleasure of skiing. Who had he met? How could it have been . . . murder?

Venus covered her ears as though she could blot out Bahira's voice. *"I've thought from the start that Jeremy's death might not have been an accident . . ."*

Forcing herself to look down, she read further, using the same method that had brought her results the first time.

There were lists of the stock purchases made. The name Olympus came up again and again.

Venus lost track of time, totally immersed in the illuminating information contained in the notebooks. Jeremy would name names, she had no doubt of that. At last, so many questions would be answered . . .

It had been a good idea using Eli Weldon-Tate's private elevator. Desperation had been the order of the day since so much had gone awry in Florida.

He had to get those ledgers. Everything would be in ruins if the information was made public.

The lid would be off, with little chance to recoup.

Pretty Venus Wayne didn't have the right to cause a downfall, especially after he had sacrificed so much to climb that ladder toward power and prestige. At the moment the Wayne woman was the skunk in the woodpile. After she was taken care of there were others, but first . . . Venus Wayne.

The key to the elevator had been a bonus. It had been lying on Venus Wayne's desk one day, asking to be taken. That had given him the idea to search Wayne's desk more thoroughly. He had turned up the disk, hadn't he? There might be other things there like the ledgers.

It was a heart-pounding moment, stepping into Eli Weldon-Tate's office. He wasn't there; the fates were favorable.

Turning the knob of the door down the hall and opening it a crack, he spotted Venus Wayne. She was reading from ledgers and jotting things on a pad. Could they be Teague's? What luck!

Today he would get what he wanted and send her to hell!

The job would be easier because the Wayne woman was deeply engrossed.

Pushing the door open wider and moving stealthily, he approached the woman hunched over the desk.

Good! The blow took her behind the right ear. Venus slumped forward, unconscious.

Scooping up the notebooks took no time at all. But getting Venus to her feet and back to Eli's office took a great deal of huffing and puffing and straining. Had to get her in the elevator. The Wayne woman was needed as insurance. When she wasn't needed, she would be killed. Hurry!

Once the elevator started its descent to the basement, it couldn't be stopped . . . unless Eli Weldon-Tate activated his key at the same time.

He punched a button and the door closed. They were on the way to freedom.

Venus was missing.

The minute Eli stepped from the elevator, he sensed that something was wrong. The pale look on the receptionist's face was his first warning.

"What's wrong, Deena?"

"It's Venus . . . I assumed she met up with you. She hasn't been answering her phone—and she's usually so conscientious about taking short lunches or telling me if she's going out. I—"

Eli strode down the hall before she had a chance to finish. Fear thudded through his bloodstream as he threw open the door to Venus's office.

She wasn't at her desk.

He glanced toward her computer. The machine was on and her chair was overturned. Papers, pens, and sundry supplies were scattered across the desk and onto the floor.

All at once his breathing was labored as though he was a finalist in a marathon. "Venus!"

Dismas, who had been walking by, stopped dead and stared at his nephew.

Eli saw how his uncle's face changed. "I don't know where she is, Uncle Dismas."

Dismas inhaled, relaxing a bit. "Now, my boy, surely there's no need for concern. I'm sure she's around the building." As he spoke, Dismas strode into his nephew's office, going at once to the telephone.

Before Dismas could lift it, Eli's hand was there, lifting the instrument and punching the security number. "Ed, I want all your people to report on this. I'm looking for Miss Wayne, and I need to know where she is at once. I want to hear details as soon as you get them."

Dismas studied his nephew in clinical surprise. He had never seen Eli so shaken. "She means a great deal to you, doesn't she?"

"Only the world, Uncle."

Eli's terse words touched the older man. Dismas put a hand on his arm. "She's around, my boy, surely you believe that. There's no need for such anxiety."

"There's every need." In short, sharp sentences,

Eli explained what had happened to Venus while she'd been in Florida.

"And you're sure Venus was the target the day the sniper was in the atrium?" Dismas exhaled heavily, seeing how Eli's features constricted.

Eli nodded once, cold perspiration beading his body.

"My boy! Why haven't you gotten Spider and his people in on this?"

"Tell you the truth, sir, I thought I could handle it myself."

"Well, I think we need him now." Dismas took the phone away from his nephew and dialed. "Spider, get some people and come over to Weldon-Tate's at once."

Eli paced the office, going into Venus's office now and then and glaring at the phone.

It was during one of his many prowls through Venus's office that he paused to look at her desk. Her notepad was on the floor next to her bag, almost hidden by other papers.

Leaning down, Eli looked into the open handbag. The ledgers were gone! Damn! Why hadn't he hired some experts to go over them? Maybe by now they would know why they were so important and to whom. His hand clenching around the notepad, Eli straightened, his breathing labored.

"What is it?" Dismas asked, glancing over the mess. "Is that Venus's writing? What are those notations about Olympus?"

"What?" Eli stared down at the pad in his hand, reading each word. "It would seem her partner feared for his life," he murmured. He read some of the scribbles on the paper. "What's this? A member of the Weldon-Tate board who's always on the

Olympus board? Why would Venus's partner mention that? Unless—"

"Unless it was very important to him." Dismas hurried through to Eli's office. "Let's run these account numbers through the computer and find out who they belong to."

Eli sat down in front of Venus's computer, punching up the portfolios mentioned in the ledger.

The two men worked quickly.

Eli input the numbers as quickly as he could. File after file turned up nothing—dead ends. Then one name appeared.

Dismas sat down suddenly in a chair near Eli. "Eli . . ."

"I see it, Uncle. Benedict James is not only on the board, he's the president of Olympus. And look at the trading he's been doing. Those notebooks I told you about might be the reason she's . . . she's not here. They must contain some very damaging information about Benedict."

"They were her partner's, weren't they?" At Eli's nod, Dismas sighed. "Was the partner into the same kind of fast-lane stock dealing that brought on Black Monday?" Again Eli nodded. Dismas shook his head. "Do you think she was taken? Kidnapped, Eli?"

"It's a possibility. I do know she was being followed. Her life has been threatened too many times." Eli hit the desktop with his closed fist. "If she's in danger . . . if it's Benedict—"

"Don't jump the gun, Eli."

"I never had an inkling that Benedict was on the board of Olympus. Why didn't that ever come up in conversation? We'd discussed Olympus many times. Why didn't I think to look into his personal dossier until now?"

"Why would you? There's never been reason to doubt Benedict, though he has always been ambitious," Dismas mused. "His father worried about that." The older man shifted in his chair. "More than once he told me he thought his son was obsessive about money and power." Dismas shrugged. "Not that it means anything."

Eli studied the green figures on the computer screen. "If I were discredited and ousted from the board of Weldon-Tate, Benedict could rise up and—"

"Do you think he aspired to be CEO of Weldon-Tate?" Dismas asked.

"I don't know and I don't care. But I have a feeling that Benedict James has abducted Venus." Eli leaped to his feet. "We have to find him," he said, grabbing the phone receiver with barely restrained violence.

When Spider arrived, Dismas said, "You were speedy. Did you bring some people?"

"Yes, sir, I did. They're waiting downstairs."

"What the hell . . . ?"

Dismas looked back at Eli. "What is it?"

Eli stared at the phone in his hand. "Benedict's secretary says he's gone for the day . . . and he isn't at home, either."

"Easy, my boy, we'll find her."

Swiveling, Eli stared at the inscrutable Spider. "Venus Wayne could be in trouble. We have to find her."

Spider nodded.

Eli was about to say more when the phone rang at his elbow. He picked it up on the first ring, his voice harsh. "Has anyone seen anything of Benedict James? They did? He was leaving? Ed, what time was this? Okay. What was he driving? A black

Caddy with tinted windows?'' Eli dropped the
phone back into the cradle. "Dammit, he's out
there, and I know he has her!" His skin crawled
with the certainty that Venus was in peril. "Where
the hell is Benedict?" Staring at Spider for a moment, he leaned down and scribbled an address.
"Have some of your people go there and look for
James."

"Will do." Spider went to another phone and
spoke briefly. Then he approached Dismas. "No
sense me waiting around. We'll sniff around the
building on our own."

"Good idea." Dismas held up the printout con-
taining information on Benedict James. "I want
someone on this man. I want to know the labels on
his drawers, the kind of shaving cream he uses.
Understood?"

Spider nodded and slipped out the door.

The phone rang several times with varying reports. Eli's anger turned into rock-hard tension,
his eyes glittering dangerously.

"Steady, my boy," Dismas warned.

Eli glared at his uncle. "I have to find her,
Dismas. I love her!"

Chapter Ten

Venus's mouth was like the bottom of a bird cage. Bile rose in her throat. Pain shot through her head when she tried to lift it, and her eyelids were lead weights.

The motion of the car was making her sick. Car? Forcing her eyes open, she had a moment of panic. She couldn't see. When she reached up to rub her eyes, her hands wouldn't move. I'm tied, she thought stupidly, and realized that her mouth was gagged, too.

As hard as she tried, she couldn't seem to shift away from the choking odor. Her cramped body had her groaning in protest.

Cold penetrated her body and mind, and she began to shiver.

Feet and hands numb with frost and lack of circulation, she tried to force her mind to focus on other things, to think.

What was she doing in the car? Had she been knocked unconscious or was that another aberration? Where was she? Moving her tied legs she thumped against a wall? Not a wall. It had to be an automobile. Could she just be suffering from vertigo? Trying to hunch into a more comfortable position, she raised up and bumped her head.

She was in the trunk of a car! That was why she

felt the motion, smelled the fumes. Whose car? Why?
Don't panic, she thought. Fear threatened her, causing her breathing to become ragged. Every breath
seemed poisonous. Stop! Think. Venus knew she
couldn't help herself by falling apart.

She didn't know how long she was jostled and
jounced, but the nausea increased from the fumes
in the enclosed area. Venus had to fight it. Humming songs in her mind, she tried to distract herself.

By the time the car stopped, she was semi-conscious.

"That's right, Miss Wayne, don't talk. You might
inhale that gag and kill yourself."

The silky laughter was alien . . . yet familiar.
Did she know the kidnapper? Roughly lifted from
the trunk, Venus banged her leg against something
metal that she assumed was the bumper. Her groan
of pain was smothered by the gag.

"You're heavier than you look."

Venus sagged when her legs hit the pavement,
her numbed ankles stinging when the rope at her
feet was removed so that she could walk. She stumbled along at the side of her captor. When she
heard the humming sound, she knew they were in
an elevator. Were they in an apartment building?
Had anyone seen her arrive?

"There, stay there."

Venus fell forward with the thrust at her back,
stumbling to her knees.

"Stay still. I'm going to tie your ankles again.
Stop shaking your head. You're going to be tied."

Minutes later she was alone again, lying on the
floor, trussed like a chicken. Forcing herself not to
panic, she hunched along on her back, trying to
find a wall or solid object so she could raise herself.

When she struck a hard substance, something
sharp scratched her face. Moving her head cau-

tiously, she found the pointed object again, angling her head so that the blindfold hooked there. Then she strained upward. Slowly the cloth moved downward and she could see.

It took her eyes several minutes to adjust to what seemed like a flood of light, though it was only sunlight filtering through the grimy window.

Venus felt a rip down her skin as she desperately tried to free herself from the gag, the spike catching her cheek and tearing. When the material finally loosened, settling off her mouth onto her chin, she sobbed in relief, gulping great breaths of oxygen. For several minutes there were dancing spots in front of her eyes and her body was chilled with cold perspiration.

Pulling herself together, Venus looked around her, trying to orient herself. Was she in a garage? A shed? A warehouse? Where? Who was holding her here? And for what reason?

"We have to find him, Uncle." Dismas dissected every bit of information they had on Benedict, going over it again and again. "I've got to think like him."

"If he's our man, and it looks like he is, his mind is a corkscrew, Eli. It won't be easy tracking him." Dismas sipped the hot black coffee that had been brought to them by Eli's secretary.

One of the men had discovered that Benedict James did indeed own a black Cadillac with tinted windows, exactly like the car that had nearly hit Eli and Venus in the underground parking garage. As the car had once belonged to his father, Benedict rarely used it.

"Think, Uncle, think," Eli urged after he'd gotten off the phone with the police. "Where would he take her? We might not have much time."

"I'm trying." Dismas sat behind Eli's desk, steepling his hands in front of him. "We checked all Ben's properties and none seem likely—"

"Wait!" Eli leaned across the desk, fixing his uncle with a hard stare. "What if some of his properties are still listed under his father's name? As his father's sole heir, they would be at his disposal."

Dismas exhaled. "All right. Let's go with that. I knew a little about Julian's holdings."

"Why do you look like that, Uncle. You're gray. Tell me."

Dismas shook his head as dark memories washed over him: Julian's frequent complaints about Benedict's behavior, his disappointment in his only son, his fears about the selfish, ruthlessly ambitious nature of young Benedict. Julian and Benedict hadn't been close in the last years of the older man's life, but Dismas had just assumed it was father-son antipathy. He licked his lips. "I should have given Julian's words more credence. He said that at times when Benedict started in his law business they had fierce arguments about ethics . . . at one time Julian said he feared for his life." Dismas's words trailed off. "Julian's death was very sudden, Eli, but it never occurred to me . . ."

The older man faltered, shaking his head, his eyes going to his nephew. "We have to find Venus."

"Think, Uncle. Did Julian have a special place he owned that might be unknown to most people?" Eli quizzed abruptly, his face tight and gray-hued.

Dismas shook his head. "It's been years . . ." He paced up and down, scratching his chin. "There was a place, Eli, an old warehouse that had been Julian's father's. Julian said he'd never sell it, that he kept the firm's archives in there. I'm not sure I can find it, but I'll try."

"Let's go."

Eli wasted no time with stoplights, caroming through traffic like a battering ram. "Keep talking, Uncle. If it's near the river and you have some idea of the location, we'll find it. We have to!"

The going was slow in the warehouse district, but then Dismas pointed a shaking finger. "I'm almost sure, Eli."

Eli slammed on the brakes and jumped out of the car.

Dismas was at his heels when the two entered the warehouse. "Wait for me, nephew."

Eli took deep breaths as he looked around him, eschewing the ancient elevator and opting for the stairs. As he hesitated, he heard a scuffling sound on the second floor of the cavernous wooden structure. Turning to his uncle, he gestured toward the wall phone. *Call the police*, he mouthed.

Turning away, Eli began the long, careful climb to the second level of the building, a good twenty feet above. What made him sure that Venus was up there? Intuition?

Step by slow step, he ascended the wide staircase.

Benedict James entered the room where he'd been keeping Venus. He was shocked to see that she had managed to get the gag out of her mouth and that she was sawing away at the bindings on her arms. Even as he watched, one of her arms dropped forward. Pretty little Venus Wayne. "That's enough, Miss Wayne."

"You! Why have you brought me here?" Anger superseded fear as she stared at Benedict.

"If Jeremy Teague had had your gumption, we

might have come through Black Monday smelling like a rose. But he caved in, contacted the State Attorney General's Office. He wanted to clean the slate and start again."

"He did?" Venus responded slowly, rubbing her swollen and reddened wrists. When she saw his twisted smile, she groaned. "*You* did something to his brakes. Damn you! Why?"

"My dear Miss Wayne, surely that's obvious. I *am* Olympus Corporation. If he had pointed the investigators my way, it would have destroyed a life's work. I arranged to meet him at the ski resort, then fixed the brakes on his car. If I wouldn't let my own father interfere with my plans, I surely wouldn't let Teague. He was useful for a while, but . . ." Benedict shrugged.

Venus's mind raced. Was he saying he'd killed his own father? "Your father?"

"My father was an interfering miser with no vision! Just because he was content with the status quo, he tried to make me kowtow as well." Benedict waved his arm. "This place was one of his refuges. And I'm going to burn it down when I take over Weldon-Tate!"

"When are you going to do that?" Venus slyly looked around her, searching for a handy weapon. If only she'd managed to untie her ankles.

"When Eli is put in jail. I've salted enough files to prove him culpable of illegal stock trading." Benedict frowned. "I'd prefer him dead, but that might bring investigations that could uncover too much. Dismas Weldon would never rest if something happened to his beloved nephew." Benedict looked puzzled. "So many people are devoted to Eli."

"Dismas wouldn't suspect you of anything, would he?" Venus tried to bend down to loosen her bonds.

"Stop that! Do you think you're fooling me? Trying to keep me talking while you free yourself. Don't waste your time, Venus Wayne. You aren't leaving here."

"Are you the one who fired the gun in the atrium?" The question was a shot in the dark, a ploy to distract him.

"Very good, Miss Wayne. And I almost got you that day . . . and Eli. Actually, I couldn't believe my luck. I knew Eli was going down to the lobby. He was my target at that moment. I wasn't worried about you then. What a coup when the two of you were together! It would have looked like another distraught investor striking back." Benedict frowned. "I shouldn't have missed. Did you know that there were other times that I was near you?"

Venus stared at him nonplussed. Was he mad or vicious or both? A movement in the outer corridor caught her eye. Was that a shadow on the wall? Was someone there?

"Were you Pluto?" Venus almost didn't care. Buying time was important. Maybe Eli would find her.

"Bingo, again, Miss Wayne. You aren't quite the dummy I assumed you were, partnering with a man like Teague."

"Do you have the ledgers?"

"Yes, I do, and they will be burned . . . as well as you and the building."

"Benedict, did you do this all on your own? I must say I'm impressed."

"Let's say I had a little involuntary help from staff people. They thought all the files they brought to me were to clear Eli's name. I used them, instead, inserting information that will incriminate Eli." Benedict looked down at the ledgers he'd put on a nearby table. "I searched for these in your apartment."

"You're the one who ransacked it," Venus said, keeping her voice neutral. "And were you at the park in Florida, too?"

"Yes. How did you like the alligator?"

Venus fought the bile that threatened to rise in her throat. "Were you the woman who pushed me into traffic?"

"Right again." Benedict shook his head. "A woman with an analytical mind. My mother had no mind at all," he said scathingly. "No one recognized me in Florida. You were lucky that day, too."

Venus stiffened when his eyes fixed on her again, his glance going from her head to her toes.

"You are rather pretty, Miss Wayne. Pity you didn't stay out of the way. None of it had anything to do with you. If you'd minded your own business and mailed those ledgers to me, you might have been home free."

Venus saw another flicker of movement in the hall and had to force her eyes from it. "How did you gain control of Olympus?"

Benedict's wide smile was a cold, raw wind that froze the blood. "There are a few persons in the right places who owe me favors. I made sure of that. Brick by brick, I built my power base. Bit by bit, things began to snowball and grow. I planned every move."

There was another sound. Venus watched Benedict James turn and start for the door. She had to warn whoever was out there.

Eli heard the bloodcurdling scream and recognized Venus's voice. Anger and fear boiled into rage inside him. With the cry that he and his men had used when he'd been a young squad leader in Vietnam, he threw his body against the door. In a tight roll, presenting the smallest target, he was in the room.

"Eli!" Venus screamed, flinging her body toward Benedict. She had to reach him, stop him, though her feet were still tied to the stanchion.

She didn't reach her target, but it was enough to distract Benedict and give Eli the edge he needed.

"Damn you, Eli," Benedict growled. Then he aimed the gun.

Eli's body fired through the air like a missile, striking the other man, knocking the gun from his hand and taking him to the floor.

Over and over the two men went, struggling to get in a blow.

"Eli!" Venus groaned, trying to crawl to him.

Out of breath, Dismas staggered through the door, taking in the situation in a glance, then moving toward Venus.

"Wait, wait, Venus, let me help you." Eli's uncle lifted her and removed her bonds. "Be careful, Venus. I've called the police. They're on the way."

Before Dismas could reach the two men, Eli drew back his fist. The crack of bone meeting bone was unmistakable. Benedict groaned, then sagged and collapsed against his adversary.

"Eli, Eli . . ." Venus crawled toward him.

He turned, releasing Benedict and rushing toward her. "Venus! You're bleeding. Are you all right?"

"Yes, yes. Eli, I need you!" she sobbed, her hands outstretched.

"Darling." He reached for her, scooping her into his arms, his eyes scanning the scratch on her face.

Dismas, watching the two of them, caught a movement in his peripheral vision. Moving swiftly, he pulled a small gun from his coat and pointed it right at Benedict. "You know I'm a good shot. Don't tempt me to rid the world of a cancer, Benedict. I heard what you said about your father. You gave him something, didn't you? He didn't have a heart attack."

"Prove it," Benedict rasped defiantly.

"Not content to swindle your mother and the customers of Olympus, you tried for the whole nine yards ... including Weldon-Tate. What an egotistical dog you are!"

"I was meant to have it! You and your stupid nephew with all your money didn't have a clue on how to spend it, how to make it grow."

"You're forgetting the losses you took on Black Monday."

"That would have been absorbed by the monies that were coming in from investors. I made money!"

"By collusion and chicanery. Damn you, you'll pay, not only with money, but with time in prison— for murder! You've been found out." Dismas pointed a finger at Benedict. "You killed your father and Jeremy Teague. We'll find proof. I'll put my people on it."

"They won't find anything."

"Your father was my close friend," Dismas said solemnly. "My people will find something."

Soothed by Eli's nearness, Venus waded through the barrage of questions from the authorities. But after a time, fatigue took over and everything started to run together. Her words began to blur as the detective repeated questions.

"She's tired, Detective," Eli said. "I'm taking her home."

The detective nodded, watching Venus. "You will have to come to police headquarters and give a more formal statement, Miss Wayne."

"She and I will be glad to accommodate you, Detective, but I want to take her to my physician first, then she needs to rest. It's been an ordeal."

"Of course. Ah, there's one more thing. You mentioned that the accused, Mr. James, is the man who tried to kill Miss Wayne on more than one occasion. Do I understand you correctly, Mr. Weldon-Tate?"

"You do. I think when you question him, you will find that he is responsible for two murders as well."

The detective's eyes narrowed on Eli. "Those are serious charges."

"I want my lawyer," Benedict interrupted stridently.

Eli ignored him and approached a pale and shaken Dismas. "Thanks, Uncle."

Dismas shook his head. "I should have listened to his father. I might have been able to stop him earlier. Killing his own father . . ." He shook his head.

"Did Benedict admit to that?" Eli looked graven from rock, his hold tightening on Venus.

Venus shuddered. "Yes, he told me all about it."

Eli shook his head, then reached out to press his uncle's arm. "I know how close you and Julian were. I'm sorry. We'll talk later. I'm taking Venus to see a doctor."

"I'll stay here and talk to the police," Dismas whispered to his nephew, shaking his head. "This has been a nightmare."

"Hasn't it?" Eli stared across the room at the man who'd been a business and social contact for years.

"You won't get away unscathed, Eli." Benedict stared back. "There's too much evidence stacked against you."

"And you stacked it?" The harsh laughter that answered his question had Eli clenching his fist. Gritting his teeth, he turned away. "We'll see you at police headquarters, Detective." He kept his arm around Venus as they left the room and went down the long, steep staircase to the street.

Eli helped Venus into the front seat of the Rolls-Royce. She turned to him, smiling as he got behind the wheel. Then her smile faded. "What is it?" His face was rigid, his hands spasmodic on the wheel.

"You could have died. He gagged you. You said it choked you and that the fumes in the trunk were suffocating . . ."

She put her hand on his arm. "Nothing serious happened, Eli. I'm fine."

"Venus, I can't live without you. I found that out today."

She laughed shakily. "It's been a day for revelations. I found out the same thing."

The preliminary hearing for Benedict James was a shocker. The depth and scope of his many scams that were to lead him to money and power were laid open to public scrutiny.

Papers and periodicals had profiles on him.

"He was a damned charlatan," Dismas muttered as he accompanied Eli and Venus from the court hearing.

"It's a relief to know that Venus is safe now." Eli kept her close to his side.

"The trial will be a painful eye opener for all of us, my boy. Faith in my fellow man has been sadly dented."

Eli nodded.

"But I don't worry about you anymore. You'll be all right." Dismas smiled at his nephew. "More than all right, I should think." He kissed Venus's cheek. "My car is over there. Spider is driving me to my massage this morning. We're going to discuss setting him up in a detective business."

Venus watched the older man stroll toward the car.

"He's remarkable, isn't he?"

"Yes." Eli held her hand as they walked across the parking garage to the car.

For the hundredth time since her rescue, Eli wondered what preyed on her mind. Those speculative looks had increased since he'd found her in the warehouse. Yet every time he asked her what was wrong, she insisted that everything was fine.

Although they hadn't really had much time to talk about their future, Eli was now sure of one thing: he wanted to marry this woman. Now more than ever, he wanted to make her his . . . forever. She'd chased away the dark clouds in his life, and now she was free to love him . . . wasn't she?

But he needed to know what was bothering her. Why did she eye him with such an inscrutable look of fear?

One evening, shortly after the hearing, Venus entered the living room and found Eli staring out the windows at the glittering lights of Manhattan.

Tired after her long day in the office, Venus had changed into a comfortable silk dress that draped her curves in a swirl of periwinkle blue. A jumpy, reluctant feeling nagged at her as she approached him. From the troubled lines on his face, she was sure he was bearing the weight of the world. And she was doubly sure that his problem concerned her.

"Is it all that bad?" she asked in a teasing voice.

Startled, he spun around. "Venus!" His eyes ran over her hotly. "I was just thinking of you."

"Oh?" She stiffened, preparing herself for a blow. "Well, then, I guess I'm in trouble. You look worried."

His face softened when he noticed her concern. "It's not that bad. Come in . . . sit down, please." He watched the sensuous sway of her body as she moved toward him, his blood thudding through his veins.

As Venus passed him to take the seat he indicated, she felt his hand feather over her hair and down to her shoulders. "You're hair is so radiant— like liquid fire. I can't believe I almost lost you." His voice was strained, as if the thought still gave him pain.

Whirling around, her hands went out to him. "Eli, if you've changed your mind about us—about our future, I—"

"Never! Not in a million years," he growled as he hauled her against his chest. His lips met hers, touching her with a tingling flash of lightning.

Venus clung to him, lips exchanging sensual secrets, chasing away fear and doubt. When she pulled back a fraction of an inch, she couldn't lift her eyelids, which were so heavy with dazed passion. "Oh, Eli," she whispered, her body pliant and soft against his. "I guess I can't hide my heart away from you forever, can I?"

He nodded. "That's why I have to talk to you. Would you like to sit down?"

She nuzzled her lips against his neck. "Actually, I'm quite happy right here."

He chuckled against her hair. "And I want nothing more than to hold you in my arms forever. Life would be intolerable without you, Venus. I need you like I need air and water. You're sustenance to me."

"I know the feeling," she said, tightening her arms around his shoulders. "And it scares me to death."

He broke away to pour her a glass of wine, then sat down beside her on the overstuffed love seat. "From the first moment we met, I felt that I'd truly found my match—you're the only woman who's ever made my life so complete. I knew I had to have you, but I need all of you, Venus. These fences you throw up between us are driving me insane. Why can't you trust me—after all we've been through together?"

She bit her lip, genuinely moved by the pain in his eyes. "I do trust you, Eli. And I never meant to mislead you. I really thought that I'd be ready to . . . commit myself to you once the danger was over."

"Commit?" He frowned. "You make it sound as though you're going off to prison."

"Do I?" Venus shrugged. "It must be a Freudian slip. Marriage scares me, Eli. I love you desperately, but I'm so afraid I'll make a lousy wife to you!" Her violet eyes were glassy with tears. "I was orphaned at a young age and . . . and I never really knew my parents."

"I know that, darling." Eli squeezed her shoulders reassuringly. "And I know it must have been tough on you as a kid. But that's all past now."

She looked down. "I vowed to overcome those circumstances. I've spent most of my life duking it out with the world—until I met you. Suddenly, a

wonderful, indomitable man stepped into my life
and offered me protection—security—all the things
I craved as a child but never had." Two hot tears
rolled down her cheeks as she met his piercing
green gaze. "I love you, Eli, but I've been fighting
the world for so long, I don't know if I can stop!"

He gently brushed away her tears, then held her
for a long time, rocking her in silence. When her
sobs lessened, he took a deep breath and whispered in her ear. "I'm not asking you to give up
the battle, Venus." He leaned back so he could
stare into her violet eyes. "Your fierce independence—that wild, fighting spirit of yours is one of
the many things that attracted me to you in the
first place."

He smoothed back her hair, and she couldn't
help but shudder with longing.

"But next time you go to war, couldn't we at
least be on the same team?" His eyes gleamed
with loving mirth.

"You rascal," Venus said, her voice still hoarse
with tears. "Is this marriage thing negotiable? I
mean, you don't expect me to give up my career
and learn how to boil water and fetch your slip-
pers and all that?"

He laughed. "Is that why you were feeling
trapped?"

After a moment's thought, she nodded. Venus
knew she could be happy living under Eli's loving
protection—but only if she didn't have to fill the
mold of a corporate wife, which just wasn't her.

"Well, let's see," he said. "Weldon-Tate will certainly benefit from your contribution, Monihan is
great at boiling water, and I don't even *wear* slip-
pers!" He wiped at the tears on her cheeks and
gently kissed the tip of her nose. "And if and when

the little Weldon-Tates come along, we'll hire a nanny to keep them in line."

"A houseful of baby investors." Venus sighed. "That'll be something to see."

"So . . ." Eli's tone was all business now. "Do we have a deal? Will there be a merger?"

Venus nibbled at his earlobe then gazed at him thoughtfully. "I'll have to read the fine print of the contract, of course—"

"Of course."

"But, based on this session, I would say we have a deal, Mr. Weldon-Tate."

"Ummm . . ." Eli trailed moist kisses along her neck.

Under the heat of his lips, Venus felt as though she were melting. "However," she murmured, "I'm afraid we'll have to have lots of these negotiating sessions."

"Lots of sessions . . ."

"Though I'm warning you, I drive a hard bargain."

"A hard bargain . . ."

"I love you. And I adore whatever it is you're doing to my neck." Venus sighed and surrendered herself to the fires within, passions inflamed by Eli's touch. "And as long as I'm your wife, I promise to do my best to make this marriage a good investment," she teased.

Eli swept her into his arms and paused for a fraction of a second to glimpse the hunger in her violet eyes. "That's one investment I'd bet my life on!"

The End?

The end of a book is never really *the end* for a person who reads. He or she can always open another. And another.

Every page holds possibilities.

But millions of kids don't see them. Don't know they're there. Millions of kids can't read, or won't.

That's why there's RIF. Reading is Fundamental (RIF) is a national nonprofit program that works with thousands of community organizations to help young people discover the fun— and the importance—of reading.

RIF motivates kids so that they *want* to read. And RIF works directly with parents to help them encourage their children's reading. RIF gets books to children and children into books, so they grow up reading and become adults who can read. Adults like you.

For more information on how to start a RIF program in your neighborhood, or help your own child grow up reading, write to:

RIF
Dept. BK-1
Box 23444
Washington, D.C.
20026

Founded in 1966, RIF is a national non-profit organization with local projects run by volunteers in every state of the union.

*Love stories so promising they
could only be . . .*

Now and Forever

MAURA SEGER
Summer Heat

Gavin McClure's appearance
on her porch immediately angered
Josie Delmar. After a morning of
dealing with ranch hands and cattle,
she has no time for another city slicker.
And, she is no less pleased when she
heard *he* was her silent partner—and
determined to stay on "their" ranch! Yet
when Gavin trades his city image for
boots and saddle, Josie finds her heart
warming, and his tender kisses and
strong arms soon have her growing
weaker by the minute . . .
ISBN: 0-517-00804-1 $2.95

COMING
IN
DECEMBER!

LOOK FOR THESE NEW TITLES FROM PAGEANT BOOKS!

SUMMER LOVE MATCH
Marjorie McAneny

In tennis as in love, a challenging partner makes the game a thrilling match! But unlike tennis, where "love" means nothing, Jenny and Lance discover that love means everything in the real world.

ISBN: 0-517-00063-6   Price: $2.50

TO TAME A HEART
Aimée Duvall

Keeping a relationship strictly professional is tough when a handsome scientist tangles with his feisty female researcher! Together, Chris and Joshua are an equal match for stubbornness and smarts—and even more suited romantically! From the best-selling author of more than fourteen romance novels.

ISBN: 0-517-00073-3   Price: $2.50

IN PERFECT HARMONY
Elizabeth Barrett

She swore off love—and music—until a glorious new romance reawakened the song in her heart! But if their love is to·last, Nicholas must make Catherine believe that their union will bring a lifetime of shared joy and harmony. Will Catherine put her ego on the line for the love she craves?

ISBN: 0-517-00090-3   Price: $2.50

ON SALE AUGUST !

I have spent most of my life in Rochester, New York, a lovely town chock full of writers and artists. As a child, I often daydreamed and spun fantastic yarns for my siblings. Those daydreams have never stopped.

After two years of business school and two years of college, I married and raised a family. But through the years of diapers and scraped knees, I kept writing.

I often joke that writers are like mushroom miners, digging deeper into dark holes. Putting pen to paper is a solitary, lonely task. But, thank goodness, no writer can create in a vacuum. The world offers us rich, wondrous inspiration. My husband Whitey gives me strength. He is my dearest friend, my support, my unflagging cheerleader.

My readers are another great source of support. When reminded of my success, I'm often overcome with humility. My writing career is in the hands of devoted, caring readers, the heartland of America, the soul of romance. My gratitude to them knows no bounds.

Helen M. Mittermeyer